Reclaiming Christmas

a novel

Melissa Sneed Wilson

Jan-Carol
Publishing, Inc

"every story needs a book"

Reclaiming Christmas
Melissa Sneed Wilson
Published July 2023
Little Creek Books
Imprint of Jan-Carol Publishing, Inc.

ISBN: 978-1-954978-91-1
Library of Congress Control Number: 2023940221

You may contact the publisher:
Jan-Carol Publishing, Inc.
PO Box 701
Johnson City, TN 37605
publisher@jancarolpublishing.com
jancarolpublishing.com

For my mom, Donna Sneed, also known as beloved DeeDee to her grandkids, who always makes Christmas magical and most importantly shines the light on the true reason for the season.

Chapter One

Eli Collins was looking forward to the grocery store trip with the same enthusiasm as the approaching holiday season; he couldn't wait for them both to be over. He had planned to leave the office earlier so he could avoid driving on the interstate during the bumper-to-bumper rush hour traffic, but he got caught in a meeting that ran twenty-seven minutes over the allotted time. Not that he was counting. The meeting could've been an email, but when the marketing manager got an idea in her head, she wanted to let everyone know it.

Despite the occasional annoyance, there was something so satisfying about helping companies trim their budgets and restructure their organizations. Oftentimes the employees were too involved to be able to make the tough decisions. Not Eli, though. It was all business to him. All about the bottom line.

This was his fourth assignment this year and his favorite so far. Harbor Ridge was a picturesque city in southwest Virginia near the Blue Ridge Mountains and several small lakes. The best of both worlds. But only seventy thousand people now called Harbor Ridge home; that number had been steadily decreasing over the last five years as residents moved to bigger cities with more job opportunities. Eli had only been in this new job for two weeks, transferring from Nashville to be closer to his sister's family in the same city for his four month contract. His niece and nephew were growing up and when the opportunity came for him to be closer to his family, even

1

for this short assignment, he jumped at it. They were all each other had.

The Chamber of Commerce had brought in Eli as a consultant to help cut the town's budget so they could get out of the red. That would set up Eli's permanent replacement to grow Harbor Ridge, Virginia back to where it used to be. By then, Eli would be on to his next assignment.

As Eli pulled into the grocery store parking lot, he noticed a giant flashing billboard announcing the tenth anniversary of the Harbor Ridge Hospital's Festival of Trees & Live Nativity. Way too tacky for his taste, but they'd succeeded in drawing attention to their festival. By the time it started, he'd be on a plane to Colorado to ski with some of his college buddies. He made a mental note to investigate how much the city was spending on the event and how successful it was. At the very least they could stop the atrocious billboard. Every penny counted.

After parking and locking his dark blue Tesla, Eli slid his keys into his coat pocket and pulled out his black leather gloves. He narrowly avoided a patch of ice in the crowded parking lot as he made his way to the front of the store. The familiar sound of bells ringing signaled the Salvation Army workers. Eli pulled out his phone and pretended to be in the middle of an important text to avoid having to make any eye contact with the bell ringer.

"Merry Christmas!"

The voice was bubbly, enthusiastic and came from someone who had probably eaten one too many candy canes. He couldn't help but look up from his phone now. His eyes met with a woman, who smiled back at him. Her straight dark brown hair, tucked underneath a Santa hat, fell to the top of her shoulders, her blue eyes sparkled like the glitter on her silver sweater. He gave her a brief nod as he walked past her.

While making dinner for one could have its challenges with leftover ingredients, Eli loved to cook. One of his earliest memories with his mom was sliding the heavy wooden kitchen chair over to the counter to join his mom and *help* her with dinner. She'd been so patient with him over the years, and not just with cooking. He smiled at the memory.

He grabbed one of the last shopping carts. As he rounded the corner to the produce section, he became stuck between a restocker and a family with several children blocking his path to the Brussels sprouts. Eli tried to maintain a strict diet and he didn't stray from his shopping list no matter how frustrating the other shoppers could be.

As Eli left the grocery store, he grabbed the four bags from the buggy and left it by the cart return. He made a mental note to sign up for grocery delivery for next week. He noticed the same woman still ringing the bell with a big smile on her face as she hummed along to "Santa Claus Is Coming to Town." *Couldn't these people wait until after Thanksgiving to start the Christmas music? What kind of people didn't celebrate Thanksgiving first? Ungrateful people, that's who.* His eyes stayed on her a little bit longer this time. *She would've looked so much cuter if she hadn't been wearing that ridiculous Santa hat.*

A little boy around the same age as his nephew slowly walked up to the red bucket and dropped in a folded bill. She bent down to his level. "Thank you so very much. Merry Christmas!"

The little boy beamed with pride and ran over to his mom to enter the grocery store, nearly bumping into Eli. He looked down at the energetic little boy and smiled for the first time that hectic afternoon. He was looking forward to seeing his nephew and niece soon.

He popped the trunk to set his bags in the car, relieved to be set with groceries for the following week. One more thing off his list before three more things were added. His phone dinged with an email notification and he sat for a few minutes responding to emails. As a consultant to the city manager, he was constantly putting out small fires brought to his attention from his secretary.

He put the car in reverse and slowly took his foot off the brake, easing out of his parking spot. He looked down at his phone. In that split second, he heard a crunch as he was jolted forward, his seat belt pushing him back.

Eli couldn't believe the luck. His trip to the grocery store was about to become much longer than he anticipated.

Chapter Two

Natalie's hands couldn't stop shaking as she opened her car door. She stood up and was immediately face-to-face with the driver of the other vehicle. She recognized him from the store. He didn't give her the time of day and was buried into his phone as he walked by. It wasn't hard to tell where his priorities were. He seemed to have a one-track mind and almost like he was living life on autopilot. There was no joy that came from his eyes; they looked glazed over, almost as if he lived life through his screen. He ran his fingers through his blonde hair- what was left of it anyways.

"Are you all right?" his light hazel eyes filled with concern as he put his hand on her shoulder.

Natalie nodded. "And you?"

He rubbed the side of face over his stubble. "You didn't see me there or what?"

Obviously, you didn't see me. Natalie wanted to say but she bit her tongue.

The other driver walked around the trunk of his blue Tesla. This must have been the third time he did so. He looked up in Natalie's direction, shaking his head in disgust. "Do you have any idea how expensive this car is?" He exclaimed loudly as he threw his hands up in the air.

"Well then you shouldn't have backed into me," Natalie said. Usually soft-spoken, she wasn't about to let this accident be blamed on her. It had been a long day starting with a six a.m. exercise class, her part-time shift at the hospital, and then bell ringing for charity. Natalie looked at her watch.

4

She was going to be late for babysitting Quinn. She needed to give Hannah a heads up.

"I didn't back into you," Eli said as he looked up from his phone.

Natalie crossed her arms. "You sure you weren't on your phone?"

He shook his head before putting the phone in his pocket. "No, I was not."

Beep.

Her eyes looked down at his jacket pocket. He held her stare. *Beep* again. "Are you going to get that?"

She'd never been in an accident before and hadn't been sure what to do. Thankfully, one of the security guards from the grocery store had noticed and came out of the building to offer assistance right away. She appreciated the guard's kindness, as well as his making sure the other driver didn't leave the scene. Her arms were sore from ringing the bell for over an hour. She put her wrist in her hand and rotated it before going back to writing down the information. The administrative team at Harbor Ridge Hospital had signed up for volunteer hours as a part of their service project. Natalie finished writing down her information and she handed the card to the officer who was making a report.

"Sir, I'm going to need for you to calm down," the police officer warned, closing his book. "It seems as though it was an accident, plain and simple. You both will have to settle with your insurance companies. Good day," he said.

As she walked back to her car, she looked at the brand-new dent in her bumper. *It doesn't look too bad,* she thought. Natalie got back into her car. She unzipped the black CD pouch she'd had since high school. It had held up surprisingly well to be over fifteen years old. She picked her favorite Christmas album, popped it in the CD player, one of the perks she enjoyed from having an older car, and started singing along as she slowly backed out once again.

Natalie made a quick pit stop at her townhouse to put her groceries away. She had planned on having more time, but needed to get over to Hannah's.

She pulled into the driveway of Hannah's house at the end of the cul-de-sac. She got out of her car and walked around to the back of the car, slowly inspecting the damage again. But she was determined to put it out of her mind until she finished babysitting so the kids wouldn't pick up on her bad attitude. They were little sponges, after all.

As she was nearing the front door, she noticed the blue Tesla pulled in right behind her damaged bumper. *Oh, no. Did he follow her?* Her stomach fell to her feet as her heart thumped out of her chest. She banged on the front door with such force the pine needles from the Christmas wreath fell to the porch below.

The sound of the deadbolt unlatching relieved Natalie's nerves. Hannah opened the front door, pulled Natalie inside, and shut it and locked it again. Natalie moved into the kitchen with Hannah following behind.

"Calm down. What's going on?" Hannah asked.

No one ever calms down by being told to calm down, Natalie thought. She took a deep breath.

"The guy who hit my car at the grocery store was very irate, a real hot-head, and he's in the driveway." Her voice was still high-pitched.

Hannah grabbed her cell phone that had been charging on the kitchen counter and dialed 911. She peeked out of the curtains in the living room—then started laughing. In between breaths, she mustered, "There's been a mistake. I'm sorry. Goodbye."

Hannah reached for the deadbolt to unlock the door. "Eli . . ." Natalie heard Hannah say as she hid in the kitchen.

"You know him?" Natalie asked, her heart still racing, still keeping her distance from Eli.

Hannah smiled. "Yes, for my whole life. He's my twin brother." She turned to him, "Eli, meet my friend Natalie, the kids' babysitter."

Eli, still wearing the same dismissive look on his face, gave Natalie a brief nod before turning back to Hannah. "We've met. At least our cars have. She rear-ended me in the grocery store parking lot, but I'm sure she already told you that. Such a great 'welcome to Harbor Ridge for my first week in town.'"

Natalie moved closer to them, the beads of sweat on her forehead still visible. "I rear-ended you? That's not how I remember it."

"Well then, your memory must be just as bad as your driving."

Natalie rolled her eyes. "I thought you said your brother wasn't moving to Harbor Ridge until after the New Year?"

Eli jumped in to answer. "That was originally the plan, but then the city had some turnover with a few employees and asked if I would consider starting my job sooner. So here I am."

Hannah pushed against Eli's shoulder while giving him the kind of look a mother would give her misbehaving child "What are you doing here?"

Eli pointed to the soccer calendar on the crowded refrigerator. "Picking up Luke for soccer practice like you asked me to."

Hannah brought her hand to her forehead. "Oh right, I forgot. My days have been all messed up since going back to work. Good thing Natalie is here to keep me straight on the kids' activities."

Eli turned Hannah away from Natalie. "I didn't know you had a babysitter? I'd be happy to help with the kids when you need me."

Natalie was taken aback by how much Eli seemed to care about his niece and nephew. The guy she spoke with in the parking lot didn't seem to care about anyone except himself.

And his Tesla, of course.

"With Ben traveling so much for work and my schedule at the hospital. I needed some part time help. Besides, I thought you'd be busy getting settled?"

"There's not much for me to unpack. I'm here if you need me." He smiled at her warmly.

"Thank you." Hannah let out a deep breath.

Luke, a lively eight-year-old boy, ran into the kitchen, nearly slamming into Eli. The two of them favored each other genetically. Blond hair and hazel eyes with just a hint of mischief.

"Uncle Eli!" Luke exclaimed while holding his black and white soccer ball under his right arm.

"Hey buddy." Eli hugged Luke and playfully tried to take his soccer ball. Natalie couldn't help but smile at the way the two of them were interacting. Like two peas in a pod.

Hannah checked the clock on the microwave. "I'm going to be late for my shift. I've got to run." She turned back to Eli, "Thank you." To Natalie, she added, "Quinn is playing upstairs in her room. She's been looking forward to seeing you all afternoon."

"Me too. See you tonight." Natalie nodded.

As Natalie walked up the stairs, she noticed a family picture she had somehow missed. There was Eli, plain as day. But Hannah didn't talk about her family as much. All Natalie knew was that Hannah and her family had moved to Harbor Ridge when Hannah was in grade school. She looked back at the picture. It was of Hannah and Eli in their high school cap and gown. Both had big smiles on their faces, undoubtedly excited about what was to come. Natalie wondered how much Eli would be sticking around. She hoped he wouldn't take her place with the kids. Where had he been the last few years anyway? Maybe she'd get the chance to ask him.

Chapter Three

"It doesn't look too bad," Hannah said as she walked along the perimeter of his car. Easy for her to say. Hannah had lots of strengths, but being a car aficionado wasn't one of them.

Eli shook his head. "Just another thing to add to my to-do list I wasn't planning on." He looked back at Hannah and Ben's house. "Are you sure you want that girl hanging around your kids? Please tell me you don't let her *drive* the kids anywhere."

"Woman, not 'girl.' Eli. Come on."

He knew he had gone too far. Hannah wasn't going to let him easily off the hook. Hannah smiled slyly.

"Didn't you back into Mom's car when it was parked in the driveway our senior year?"

Eli shook his head. "This was different. Natalie should have checked her rearview mirror before she jumped on the gas."

"As opposed to Mom's car which was literally sitting still in our driveway."

"It was supposed to be in the garage. I didn't know it was there." Eli mumbled.

"Why didn't you check the rear-view mirror? And maybe Natalie thought you were pulling forward or sitting still. It's just a car, Eli. It can be fixed."

"I'm ready to go!" Luke chimed in from the backseat.

"If you can't take him tonight, he can stay with Natalie and Quinn."

"Nooo." Luke protested from the backseat.

Eli smiled at his nephew. His first smile all afternoon. This was the bright spot about moving to Harbor Ridge. Hanging out with his little buddy.

"No, I'll take him."

"Thank you." Hannah gave Eli a hug. "Lori Harrison, Nick's mom, will bring Luke home. We trade off every week."

"Great and you're welcome. I'm going to try and take my car into the body shop first thing tomorrow. When is Ben getting home?"

"Day after tomorrow." Hannah shrugged.

Eli knew all of Ben's work travel had been taking its toll on Hannah.

"Are things still going okay with you two?"

Hannah nodded. "We're working it out. Day by day. Week by week. We're definitely in a much better place than last year, that's for sure."

"I know it hasn't been the easiest past few years for you."

"For any of us, really."

Eli nodded in agreement.

"I really do appreciate you coming to help us."

"Of course. I don't think you'll need to keep having Natalie come by."

"The kids adore her and she's a great friend to me. Like a sister. I had forgotten what having one felt like."

Eli sighed. He wanted to remind her that they still *had* a sister and that he was hopeful they could all be close again, but he had tried too many times to get them to reconcile. Grief had made them grow apart.

"It's too bad you and Natalie met like you did," Hannah said. "I think you'd like her."

"Yeah right."

Hannah's shoulders dropped and he immediately sensed how much she needed him and Natalie to get along. She had been through enough the past few years. "I guess if Quinn and Luke like her, maybe she's not too bad." She was kind of cute. Except for that over-the-top glittery silver sweater she was wearing.

Hannah blew a kiss to Luke, then waved as Eli pulled out of the driveway—past Natalie's car with its dented bumper. He felt his blood pressure rising. He looked in his mirror and saw Luke's big green eyes glance up at him. They pulled up to a stop sign. Eli turned around.

"Fist bump?"

Luke held out his hand in a tight fist.

Their hands made contact and Eli made an explosion noise.

Luke's giggles filled the back seat. Eli couldn't help but smile as he turned around in his seat.

He forgot about his dented bumper.

Chapter Four

The next morning, Natalie slid her purse under her desk and turned on her monitor. She sunk back in her chair as she waited for her computer to boot up. She took a sip of coffee from her favorite mug she kept at work. She was careful to keep it far away from her keyboard. During her first week on this job, three years ago, she'd accidentally knocked over a full mug of coffee on her keyboard and had to call IT to get a replacement. For someone who liked to remain behind the scenes, becoming known as the girl who monopolized IT that day and cost the hospital a new computer had not been her best moment.

Ding.

A chat message popped up on her computer screen.

Linda Mueller was asking for the files Natalie had on the Festival of Trees. Natalie quickly copied and pasted a link to the Dropbox where she had been compiling the vendors, the food trucks, volunteers, and city permit.

Linda had more energy than the rest of the administrative team put together. She had a commanding presence, always wearing a stylish scarf around her neck. There was never a day where Linda wasn't dressed to the nines. She was the public face of the hospital when it came to special events, and she always needed to be camera ready in case the hospital needed to make a statement. That was Linda, always prepared at a moment's notice for anything that could happen.

Linda had been in her role for twenty-five years and was great at many things in her position as volunteer and special events manager, but keeping up with technology had been difficult for the almost sixty-year-old. Linda pushed on and tried her best but there was no question it was frustrating for her. Natalie was happy to help her out in the beginning but lately it seemed as though Linda had mentally checked out. Rumors had started that Linda was retiring at the end of the year. Linda was widowed a few years ago and had recently found love again.

"Want to go grab a coffee?" Rachel Murphy interrupted Natalie's concentration as she peered over the cubicle. Rachel stifled a yawn, brushing her red hair behind her ears.

"Sure," Natalie said as she stifled her own yawn.

Rachel started working the same month as Natalie. Having sat through the same weeks of endless orientation and training meetings, they'd become quick friends. Like Natalie, Rachel was single but Rachel was always up for going on a new date or trying out a new dating app. Rachel had been promoted a year ago to special events coordinator. Natalie had decided against applying; she hated getting her hopes up for anything anymore. It was better for her to play it safe and keep doing her job as an administrator. She was thrilled Rachel was able to stay in the same department as her.

"Did you see the job posting for the new volunteer coordinator?"

Natalie shrugged. Of course she had seen it. A flyer was posted in the break room for everyone to see. It was the first email in her inbox when she logged in. She deleted it without even opening the message.

"You would be fantastic for it," Rachel said as she put on her jacket and handed Natalie a folder.

Natalie slid the manila folder in its appropriate slot at the corner of her desk. She liked her desk to be organized. Everything had its place and was easy to find. The clutter could stress her out. Natalie turned back to Rachel and shook her head.

"I don't think so. I'm happy with what I'm doing now."

"Well let me know if you change your mind. I can put in a good word with Linda. Or be a reference."

Natalie shrugged again. Just then she looked up to see Hannah, dressed in her turquoise scrubs and hair pulled back, walking by the check-in desk. Hannah waved with her right hand, her left hand clutching tightly to a metallic coffee tumbler. She looked tired . . . but who didn't, at this busy time of year?

Natalie nodded back and smiled. She picked her jacket off from the back of her chair and put it on.

Rachel and Natalie walked along the hallway to the coffee shop. As they got to the coffee shop they passed the double doors that entered into the courtyard in between the three wings of the hospital. Natalie stopped and peered through the cloudy glass doors.

"Want to walk through the courtyard after we grab our coffee? The trees are gorgeous this year."

Natalie nodded. It was her favorite part of the hospital, especially during the holidays. After a few minutes after they ordered, the barista called their names and they picked up their festive coffee cups. A cold gust of air greeted her as Rachel pushed the door to the courtyard open. Natalie cupped her hands around her coffee cup and immediately felt warmth. She looked up and couldn't help but smile. She was surrounded by a hundred decorated Christmas trees. Well, 108, to be exact. Natalie and Rachel had entered each sponsor and donor into their database system and ensured the safe arrival of each tree. Each Christmas tree was sponsored by an area business or donor who decorated the tree with a certain theme. At the celebration of the Festival of Trees, the winners of the auction were announced. To read each description and application was one thing, to stand in the center of all the bright and colorful trees was enchanting. Festive Christmas music played on the loudspeakers in the background. Natalie found herself humming along. Some days, they had live musicians come and play.

Rachel turned around to her. Her arms swept across the perimeter of the courtyard. "So, which one is your favorite? Mine is the Candy Land-themed one over there." Her perfectly manicured fingernail pointed to the nine-foot tree decorated with assorted candies fixed to the tree's branches. "The Sweet Shoppe sponsored it. They always donate hot chocolate for the night, too. I wonder if they'd notice if I swipe a lollipop?"

Natalie playfully slapped Rachel's hand away. "No, you can't eat it. They're going to be auctioning off all the ornaments at the end of the season. You know that."

"I know. I know," Rachel admitted. "I just hope it doesn't go bad by then."

"I'm sure they have a back-up in case, but we don't want to get arrested. You know they have cameras installed to keep an eye on things. You could always bid on this tree."

Natalie looked at the tag. "See it says, gift baskets included 5 lollipops, a gingerbread decorating kit, assorted chocolates, and a one-hundred-dollar gift card to the store."

"Maybe I'll bid on it. Doubt I'll win on our salary though." They both laughed. They didn't get into this line of work for the paycheck, that was for sure. "You didn't tell me which one is your favorite?"

Natalie looked around. There were so many to choose from. It was tough to pick just one that stood out. In the corner of the courtyard, a tree with pink and blue lights caught Natalie's attention. As she walked closer, she noticed the tree had photo frame ornaments. Each one contained a picture of a baby who was in the NICU the previous year, and on the back was the name, the birth date, and the date they were released from the hospital. Some of the ornaments had the dates they passed away.

God be near them during this season, Natalie thought.

"We should get back for our meeting," Rachel said, glancing at her cellphone's clock.

Natalie took one last look around the courtyard. There was something very special about the community coming together to raise money for the hospital. To raise funds for the NICU families, the cancer patients, for new cures. It was an honor to get to be a part of it. Natalie was so excited for their celebration event. She and Rachel had been working on it all year and they reminisced about last year's successful festival as they walked back to their office.

Natalie sipped on her coffee as she typed away on her keyboard responding to an important email. She was too engrossed in her response to notice Linda standing over her desk, until Rachel poked her in the back.

"What?" Natalie said with a hint of annoyance in her voice.

"I'm, um, sorry, so sorry, I didn't see you," Natalie stumbled over her words.

Linda buttoned her blazer jacket. "Let's meet in the conference room. It'll be easier to spread out our materials with those long tables. We can see *exactly* where we are on things."

Natalie slowly exhaled as Linda walked away. "You could have warned me?"

"I tried. You were engrossed in your work and she probably didn't want to interrupt."

Natalie sighed. The last thing she needed was Linda to think she wasn't a team player. She looked down at her inbox and just from the morning she had three businesses deciding to not participate in the Festival of Trees Christmas event. Harbor Ridge was losing their main box stores to another town thirty minutes away that had a new flashy outdoor mall. Hard to compete with tax incentives and big new stores. Hannah had mentioned Eli had moved to Harbor Ridge to help with the economic development. She was hopeful he could make a difference for their city. They certainly needed it and Eli seemed confident in himself for sure to get it done. Part of her wondered if he'd be at Hannah's again this week.

Natalie started beating her pen against the top of her desk. They were still behind from years past but there was a month to go. This was one of the hospital's biggest fundraisers. Plenty of time to get more donations. She hoped.

Rachel turned her chair around. "What can I help you with?"

Natalie stopped beating her pen. "Oh, do I seem a little stressed?"

"I know how hard Linda is to please." Rachel raised her eyebrow, "And

I know how eager you are to people please."

"I am not." Natalie couldn't keep a straight face before cracking a smile. "Guilty as charged." It was one of the traits Natalie liked least about herself.

"Well let's figure out how to give Linda exactly what she wants."

The two ladies went to work scouring over every file they had for this year's festival.

Chapter Five

Eli woke up seven minutes before his six a.m. phone alarm sounded. He chowed down half a banana and some of a protein shake before meeting Hannah outside his townhouse. She was going to show him around the gym near his office downtown. She picked him up on her way and they rode together for the five-minute drive to the gym. On the way there they passed another billboard for Harbor Ridge's Festival of Trees celebration. They stopped at a red light directly across from the billboard. Eli couldn't hide his disgust with the ornate and flashy advertisement. "Ew. How many of these tacky billboards do they have?"

Hannah took notice of his facial expression. "I take it, you don't plan to go?"

"Why would you say that?"

Hannah laughed. Her smile relaxed as she let out a sigh before admitting. "The kids really want to go. Some of their friends from church and school are in the Christmas program."

"And you?"

"Well Christmas is still hard for me." The light turned green, and Hannah eased off the brake.

"It was Mom's favorite," Eli said.

"It was." Hannah nodded in agreement.

They continued down Market Street, where the lamp posts had been draped in white lights that would illuminate after dark. *For Sale* signs stood in the windows of several empty businesses. *Well, this is depressing,* Eli thought. No wonder the city brought him in to help bring more life to Harbor Ridge.

Eli found himself quietly reminiscing about Christmases growing up. Their mom made them so magical. He could still hear her singing "Joy to the World" every chance she got, and Nativity scenes had covered every bare counter in their house.

Hannah circled to the back lot and squeezed into a parking spot. Harbor Ridge had a lot of eager early risers. He followed Hannah around the quick five-minute tour as she showed him around the tiny gym of seven treadmills, five ellipticals, and five stationary bikes. The grips on some of the weights were peeling and it was evident that the carpet had been around since probably before they were born.

"This is it?" It was much smaller than the gym he had in Nashville. What little equipment they had seemed like it belonged in a museum. He mentally added "the gym" as a reason to look forward to his assignment after Harbor Ridge. He missed his cycle classes and looked forward to being in a bigger city where he could get back to his exercise routine again.

Hannah folded her arms. "Oh, come on. It's not that bad. You've been spoiled with your fancy gym spas and juice bars."

Eli smirked. "Don't forget the eye candy."

Hannah rolled her eyes. "Give it a chance. I always get a great workout here."

"Doing what, exactly?"

Hannah nodded toward the group exercise room. "You should try yoga or step."

"Step aerobics?" Eli laughed. "You mean like what Mom used to teach when we were kids? I remember she used to do those hilarious Jane Fonda workout videos in the living room before dinner. Remember?"

Hannah smiled at the memory and then bit her lip to control her emotion. She quickly changed the subject.

"You'd be surprised. Step aerobics is actually a tough workout."

Eli started moving side to side, exaggerating his facial expressions and movements.

"Come on, everybody. And one and two."

Hannah's laughter permeated the gym floor. Her eyes suddenly looked behind him and he turned around still wearing the goofy smile on his face.

Hannah spoke from behind him. "Eli wants to be the new step instructor."

Natalie, dressed in black workout capris and a lavender tank top, tilted her head to look at him. Eli could feel his cheeks burning red with embarrassment.

"You could have warned me we had company?" he whispered while nudging Hannah.

"You ready?" Natalie asked in Hannah's direction.

Eli pretended to be offended, "I'm not invited, huh?"

Natalie tried unsuccessfully to keep a smile at bay. "That wasn't enough of a workout just now?"

Eli took her comment in stride. "Ha ha. We'll see if I can find something to do here that's worth my time."

Natalie motioned to the group exercise room down the hall. "You don't want to join us for step class? My friend Stephanie teaches it and it starts in five minutes. I think you're warmed up now."

"Seeing how this isn't 1989, I think I'll pass. But you two have fun dancing."

"Oh we will." Natalie nodded.

Natalie's eyes rolled up toward the ceiling as she walked away, not dignifying his rejection with a response.

"That was rude." Hannah scolded him. "You could have just said 'no thanks'."

Eli scoffed. "How was that rude? You're too sensitive. Although speaking of eye candy."

His eyes followed Natalie and she walked to the exercise room in the corner of the gym and smirked.

Hannah wagged her finger at him. "Don't make me uninvite you to Thanksgiving."

Eli waved his pointer finger back at her. "Then who would make all the food?"

"Touché. I'm going to step class. I'll see you later this week?"

"Yeah sure. I can take Luke to soccer practice if you need me to?"

"Ben should be back in town, but I know the kids would love to see you whenever they can."

"Me too." Eli smiled thinking about spending time with his niece and nephew again.

Chapter Six

Natalie took her time walking to her cubicle and slowly sat down in her office chair. She let out a sigh. She should have stayed for the cool down after class instead of jetting off to the locker room and rushing back to work.

"What happened to you?" Rachel swiveled her chair around facing Natalie.

"Just tired from step aerobics. It was a tough class today." *I also had something to prove*, she thought. Every chance he got, Eli Collins was always condescending and arrogant. Whether it was about her car, which was still in the shop thanks to him, or the kind of exercise class she took, he had to let his expertise be known. His opinions that he thought were superior to everyone else's.

Rachel nodded. "Pretty soon I'm going to need to be doing some yoga or something to help with my stress from this Festival of Trees event. Linda is out of the office this week for Thanksgiving, and she left me a to-do list a mile long."

Natalie came over to Rachel's monitor, which was adorned with many colored post-it notes. "Let's prioritize what needs to be done first, what is the hardest, and then go from there. First, we need to make sure we have the city permit on record. My friend, Sandy Nelson, is handling that. Since Harbor Ridge Community Church sponsors the Live Nativity part, she always makes sure we have what we need. I'm meeting with her later this week to iron out the details on what the church is providing. Secondly, we need to confirm the staff and volunteers from the hospital. Have you checked the sign-up sheet in the break rooms yet? Do we have the contracts from the food trucks yet?"

"So many moving pieces," Rachel yawned. "I'm already tired and we have four weeks left until showtime."

Natalie yawned too. Every year felt the same way. She and Rachel stressed over how they could possibly get everything confirmed and planned, and then on December 22nd, everything came together. It was the same story every year and yet Natalie couldn't help but stress out about the festival.

Hannah walked in and waved to Natalie. "Happy Thanksgiving!" Hannah said smiling.

Confused, Natalie looked down at her calendar. "It's just Wednesday. Are you working tomorrow?"

"I'm on call. Do you have any plans tomorrow?"

"No." Natalie had already had her Friendsgiving with some people from the church's young adult ministry. She had planned to decorate for Christmas around her apartment and watch the Macy's parade like she did every year.

"Do you want to come over? We would love to have you join us for lunch tomorrow."

Natalie smiled. She had been so focused on all the work for the festival she almost forgot about Thanksgiving. Her family lived states away and she usually took time off at Christmas.

"That sounds lovely. Thank you. Can I bring anything?"

"Whatever your favorite side dish is, or a dessert? Eli's going to make the turkey."

"Oh." Natalie looked down. Of course, he would be at their family's Thanksgiving.

"Is there a problem? If you can't make it, I understand."

Natalie shuffled papers around her desk. "No, no problem. I just didn't know Eli would be coming."

Hannah nodded. "I know he can come across as kind of a jerk sometimes. He can be harsh."

Natalie didn't disagree. She'd only met the guy twice and each time he had been both insulting and demeaning. Would it really be worth it to put herself around him again? On the other hand, she knew Hannah would have her back like she did at the gym this morning.

"But he is an amazing cook," Hannah added, trying to entice Natalie to join them.

Of course, he was. He'd probably take every chance he could to let her know it, too. But a yummy meal to share with Hannah and the kids would be a nice change from the Thanksgivings she'd had in the past. On the rare occasion she wasn't working, Natalie typically ate out for Thanksgiving. She couldn't take both holidays off. This year she had gotten lucky and planned to work Friday after Thanksgiving but would be off Thanksgiving Day.

"I'll come." Natalie agreed.

A genuine smile came over Hannah's face. "That's fantastic. Quinn and Luke will be so excited."

* * *

Hannah smiled as she walked toward the elevator bank. This would be the first Thanksgiving she'd hosted in several years. All six of the dining room chairs would be occupied. Maybe this would be the year she wouldn't miss her sister as much. It was tough to not think about the what ifs when the holidays rolled around. What if they hadn't had that epic fight? What if she had kept her promise to go out to California that first Christmas instead of staying in Virginia? Thanksgiving was such an important holiday for their family growing up. The last few years though? There hadn't been much to celebrate. Maybe this year could be different. Hannah was excited to get to decorate and try to create her own special touch on it this year. Maybe she'd even try a new recipe. Or better yet, maybe she'd find a new recipe and give it to Eli. He'd always been better in the kitchen.

The elevator dinged and she stepped into chaos on the floor as she went into nurse mode. Her thoughts on Thanksgiving quickly departed her mind.

Chapter Seven

Eli stood over a pot of boiling potatoes on the stove while Hannah scattered a can of fried onion topping over the green bean casserole. It had been their mom's favorite side dish.

Five years without their parents. Five years of being orphaned. A typical fall day playing in the backyard with Luke and Quinn when a phone call shattered it all. Time had healed the jagged edges of her grief, but the pain still left a scar. Empty seats at the dining room table. Two less people to share life with.

Her kids were the ones to miss out on it most of all. Her parents had been wonderful grandparents for the time she was lucky enough to have them. Hannah and her mom were always close but Hannah's appreciation for her mother grew even deeper when she had children of her own. She never realized the amount of sacrifice and sheer exhaustion it took to raise the next generation. She would give anything to see her mom one last time so she could tell her that and how much she loved her. It wasn't fair, but she was determined to remember her parents for who they were and not how they died. And to pass on the very best of them to her kids.

Her mom had loved to cook and it was Eli who took after her in that respect. Hannah was more inclined to pick up something from a drive-thru or order-in. She was too busy to spend her time waiting for a pot to boil. Hannah did, however, inherit her mom's decorating skills. She loved beginning the first day of each month with setting out decorations for the respective holiday.

Christmas was her favorite. Or at least it used to be. This was the first year she had started the thankful pumpkin project with the kids. Her mom had done it when they were little with them. After visiting a pumpkin patch in October, Hannah took the pumpkin and put it in the center of their table. Every night after they said their blessing, she would write a word on their pumpkin for what they were grateful for. Some were funny and some were more serious.

The doorbell interrupted Eli's usual mansplaining lesson on how to cook the perfect potato and Hannah was not disappointed she had to leave the kitchen. Hannah turned the deadbolt and pulled the front door open.

Natalie, dressed warmly in her fitted black jacket and knitted pink cap, stood on their front porch holding a casserole covered in foil.

"Thanks for coming. I know the kids are so excited to have you. I am too," Hannah said, taking Natalie's casserole from her hands.

Natalie followed Hannah into the kitchen where she put down the casserole.

Natalie played with the kids in the living room while Eli and Hannah finished cooking and Ben set the table. Before long, Hannah summoned everyone to the dining room. Hannah and Ben sat at the head of the table, the kids sat across from each other as did Eli and Natalie. Hannah broke the silence.

"Ben, would you like to say grace?"

Everyone bowed their heads. At Hannah's reminder, Luke and Quinn put their hands in front of their faces.

"Heavenly Father, we thank you for this chance to be together as a family and for the food and the hands that prepared it. Amen," Ben said. "All right, let's dig in."

"Pass the potatoes," Luke asked. He looked up to Natalie and whispered with a smile. "They're my favorite." She smiled down at him as she passed the plate.

Natalie took a bite of the mashed potatoes. "Hannah, these are delicious! They may be the best mashed potatoes I've ever had. What's your secret?"

Hannah looked across the table at Eli who was beaming ear to ear. "I don't know, what's the secret, Eli?"

Natalie's face turned the same shade as the cranberry sauce.

"I'll give you the recipe later."

"Thanks." Natalie said as she looked down at the plate.

"Natalie, how long have you lived in Harbor Ridge?" Eli asked.

Natalie took a bite of a roll and swallowed. "I moved here three years ago. I met Hannah at the hospital like a year ago?"

Hannah chimed in, "Yes, it was around Halloween. We had the same costume."

Natalie continued, "Then I kept seeing her at the gym where we actually got a chance to talk because we weren't rushing to get to our place. I started babysitting the kids during the summer."

Eli set his fork down. "So, you're part-time or full-time at the hospital?"

Natalie sighed, "Currently, I'm twenty-five hours a week. Just enough for the hospital to not pay for my benefits. Ironic, right?"

Eli chimed in, "Wow that is pretty bad. So why don't you just go find another job then?"

Natalie looked down at the napkin in her lap. "Well, jobs aren't exactly easy to come by in Harbor Ridge right now."

Eli wiped his face with a napkin. "We're hoping to change that. The healthcare situation is a little more complicated though."

Natalie joked, "I guess I could just move to Canada."

Eli shook his head. "Why would you want to go live in that socialist country?"

Natalie dropped her fork on her plate, causing it to clang. "At least they care about people having health insurance."

Eli scratched his eyebrow. "I don't think you understand the economics of healthcare."

Before Natalie could open her mouth to respond, Hannah exclaimed, "Eli!"

"She started it," he mumbled.

"It's not a true family dinner without some argument about politics, right?" Ben joked, trying to diffuse the situation.

"Can we go play outside?" Quinn asked, having eaten only the dinner roll off her plate.

Hannah looked down at her daughter. "Are you sure you don't want anything else to eat?"

"Another roll?"

"Quinn!"

Eli passed his roll under the table to Quinn. He winked at Quinn, whose smile gave off the impression she was given a tremendous gift.

Natalie smiled seeing the two of them interact. Regardless of her feelings toward Eli—and so far, they had not been on good terms—there was no question he was a fantastic uncle.

"Sure, but put on your coat and gloves first. It's freezing out there."

As they were clearing the table, Hannah's phone beeped signaling she was needed at the hospital.

"You go, I'll hold down the fort." Ben said. Hannah smiled as she gave him a kiss. She walked to the front hall closet and pulled out her winter coat. As she was tying her scarf, Natalie came up to her.

"Thank you so much for inviting me for lunch." Natalie said.

"You're welcome," Hannah answered before whispering, "Sorry about Eli. He's . . . just Eli." Hannah sighed.

"That's okay, I'm used to it." Natalie smiled. She looked out the window and noticed her car was blocking in Hannah's. She grabbed her keys from the kitchen counter and her coat before opening the front door and walking to her car.

Natalie turned the key in her car, but it wouldn't start. Always the problem solver, Hannah asked Eli to give her a ride to work and Natalie a ride home.

"I could call her an Uber?" Eli said.

"I can order one myself, thank you very much." She didn't want to have to listen to any more of Eli's ill-formed opinions about her job and health-care status as if he was all-knowing about everyone and everything.

"Don't be silly, your apartment is close to the hospital," Hannah said. She turned to Eli and put on her bossy voice. "Grow up. I'm older than you, so you have to do what I say."

He held up his fingers. "Two minutes older, sis. Two minutes."

Hannah opened the car and smirked, "And don't you ever forget it."

Eli shrugged his shoulders as he opened the back door for Natalie. He walked around to the driver's side door. Natalie promptly shut the car door before letting out a sigh and then reopened it herself. She didn't need a guy, especially not one like Eli, to pretend to be chivalrous and open the door for her. Not when his demeanor the last week she had known him proved to be anything but.

Eli looked in his rearview mirror at Natalie sitting uncomfortably in his back seat. He pulled into the parking lot and up to the semi-circle to the front of the hospital and Hannah opened the car door.

"Thanks for the ride, and for all the delicious food." Hannah said.

"No problem," Eli shrugged.

"Be nice," Hannah spoke to Eli in a whisper from the corner of her mouth.

Hannah turned to Natalie. "I hope you have a great rest of your weekend. I'm glad you could join us today!"

Natalie smiled. "Thanks for inviting me."

Hannah quickly exited the car and briskly walked into the hospital.

When it was just Eli and Natalie left in the car, he looked up in the rearview mirror and noticed Natalie going through her phone.

"You can move to the front seat if you want, unless you want me to chauffeur you around?"

"If it's all the same to you I'd rather stay here away from hostile territory." Natalie said without looking up.

Eli shifted in the driver's seat. "Look, Natalie, it seems we've gotten off on the wrong foot again. I hope I didn't come across as too harsh back there. Healthcare is something I'm quite passionate about. I see it a lot in my job," he said. "Nothing personal."

"I see healthcare a lot in my job too; mainly people's lack of it. It *is* personal. For my kids and their families," she answered, still not looking up.

Natalie set her phone down and her eyes glanced up connected to his through the rearview mirror. She brought her hands together and squeezed them tightly as if to release the tension she felt before unleashing it on Eli. "There would be plenty of money for health care if it wasn't for greedy people."

"Well, we're not going to solve the world's problems today so let's just call a truce. It's Thanksgiving, after all."

"Fine," she answered as she reached for the door handle. She opened the door and climbed out. A huge chill came over the car. Eli reached over to the passenger door to open it. Natalie immediately opened the door.

"I don't live far from here, I can walk home," she said.

Eli looked down at the temperature gauge.

"It's ten degrees outside. Are you crazy?"

"I'm from Michigan. This is nothing," she said with a sneer as she walked away.

Eli sat in his car, frozen in disbelief. He was only trying to be nice, but if Natalie didn't want his help he wasn't going to beg.

Eli pulled into the garage of his townhouse. A few minutes later, Natalie walked up her driveway. Across the street.

Chapter Eight

Hannah arrived home from work after midnight and barely remembered to brush her teeth before hopping into bed. Holidays were always busy at the hospital, and since she was starting at the bottom since returning to nursing, her schedule did not have much flexibility. Still, she loved her job and being able to help her patients.

Ben slept peacefully next to her. She snuggled up next to him. These days it seemed as though they were ships passing in the night. He had been out of town earlier in the week closing a business deal. She missed having his help when he was gone.

She was looking forward to celebrating their anniversary with two nights away in a few weeks. They had come so far the past two years. They married young, right out of college. There were career changes, new cities, and navigating parenthood. At times the weight of it all felt too much.

After her parents died, Hannah bottled up her feelings. She felt numb. Numb from the investigation, numb from the double funeral they had to have.

Then one day Luke dropped her mother's jewelry box by accident and it shattered on the tile floor in their bathroom. Hannah sobbed for days over it. She hit rock bottom in her grief and there was nowhere else to go but up. She realized it was time to move forward. She got counseling and started reaching out to friends again. Well, the friends who had stuck around. It hadn't been easy to move forward, but eventually the days seemed brighter, and her purpose and smile came back. So did a desire to return to her field before kids: nursing.

As much as she loved her jobs, both being a nurse and a mom, Hannah was counting down the days for her and Ben's anniversary trip. She was desperate for a break and could feel her stamina and patience starting to wear thin. All signs pointing to the fact she needed time to regroup and recharge.

Natalie had agreed to stay over for two nights with the kids. They had planned the trip a year ago, long before Eli had made the move to Harbor Ridge.

At the time, Hannah hadn't been sure Eli was reliable enough to count on for childcare since he worked a ton of hours, but he was slowly proving her wrong.

It would be the first time they had left the kids overnight before. The kids were older now and their bedtime routines more settled. Natalie had been such a gift to their family since she started working for them earlier in the summer. It was as though she had always been a member of their family. The kids adored her and Natalie treated them like they were her own. Hannah sometimes felt jealous of her friends who had parents in town to watch their kids, who got childcare at a moment's notice. She struggled with feeling as though she didn't have enough energy for her kids, and her husband and her job. Something usually failed.

She rolled over and looked at the clock. 3:15 a.m. Three more hours until she needed to be up to get things ready for the kids to go to school.

Chapter Nine

U p before his alarm, as per usual, Eli sat his coffee cup next to his laptop. He planned to answer a few work emails before heading to the office.

He signed on to LinkedIn to catch up on some industry news. His eyes immediately glanced at the thumbnail of a beautiful and familiar woman. Against the feeling he had not to click on her profile, he couldn't help himself. Kendra had changed her last name. The temptation to find out more information was too much, he clicked on her profile. Immediately, her gorgeous headshot came up on his screen. Her long blonde hair sat on the shoulders of her black suit. A gold necklace sat above her perfectly pressed white blouse. He quickly went down the rabbit hole of searching her name online. She had gotten married the weekend before.

She was as close as he'd ever gotten to being married. They met through mutual friends when he was working his first consulting job. Kendra was a year younger than him, and they had known each other as acquaintances in college but their paths had never crossed. Once they were working together, they enjoyed attending company functions. On the rare occasion they weren't traveling for work, they enjoyed watching movies together while scrolling through their phones, but it never went much deeper than that.

The second Christmas he and Kendra were together, Kendra dropped hint after hint that she was expecting a diamond on Christmas morning. Eli wasn't ready and Kendra didn't want to wait. There was no space for compromise. He couldn't be what she needed. Hannah, whom Eli always trusted, wasn't Kendra's biggest fan. She thought Kendra and Eli were too similar to work well together and she didn't like the pressure Kendra was putting on Eli. And it turned out she was right. As usual.

He paused to wonder if things could have been different if he had just given in and proposed when she had wanted a ring. Some nights it was lonely to go home alone.

He closed out of the Internet and disconnected the Wi-Fi. This was a trick he had learned in grad school to keep himself in check when he needed to do coursework and didn't need the distraction of wanting to browse the internet. The emails could wait.

Then he opened the folder on his desktop titled "Christmas in Harbor Ridge" to go through their budget with a fine-tooth comb. Just how much was the city spending on that atrocious billboard? He was finally about to get his answer.

This was worse than he'd thought. Not only was the city hemorrhaging money across every category, but the grant they had given Harbor Ridge Community Church and the hospital had been used to fund that tacky billboard to the tune of four thousand dollars. He scrolled down to the bottom of the grant form. He hoped whoever the Festival of Trees and Live Nativity chair, Sandra Nelson was, that she was ready for some tough questions for their meeting tomorrow.

* * *

Natalie's ringing cell phone woke her up early. She'd stayed up late the night before watching back-to-back Christmas movies while drinking too much homemade hot dark chocolate with marshmallows. The chocolate had kept her up until well past one a.m. It took a few moments to wake up before she realized she could barely make out the whispering voice on the other end of the phone call.

"I'm under the weather, dear, and cannot make the meeting at the Chamber of Commerce today about our Festival of Trees," Sandy said. "Since we're co-chairs, can you go in my place? I'll email you the talking points so you can be prepared."

"Sure, I can do it," Natalie said. She would let Linda know she would be coming in late to work. "What time is the meeting?"

"Nine am. It's at city hall. Do you know where that is?"

Natalie nodded. "Yes, I do. I can walk there from the hospital. Feel better soon!"

"Thank you," Mrs. Nelson muttered before another coughing spell hit.

Natalie had been involved with the Live Nativity for three years since she moved to Harbor Ridge. Christmas was a painful season for her and the first year she attended it felt as though she got some of her Christmas sparkle back. Being a part of such a spectacular night gave Natalie a deep joy and peace. It was though every sad and hurtful memory she carried with her was transformed into something new. Volunteering at the event the following year gave her the opportunity to see that same sparkle return for others. That was why she said yes when Mrs. Nelson cornered her at church in the coffee room this year and asked her to co-chair. When Sandy Nelson asked you to do something, you didn't say anything but yes.

The unexpected bonus of volunteering with Sandy through the church was that Linda was also working on the festival and this made Natalie the perfect person to serve as the liaison between the two women. She could keep them connected and ensure that details of both events were taken care of.

After hanging up the phone, Natalie rushed to get ready for her meeting. No staying in pajamas and watching another Christmas movie this morning. She browsed her closet for the perfect outfit to wear. She wanted to be professional yet not be too dressed up for her age. She definitely didn't want to try too hard and give the wrong impression. What did one wear to a meeting with the city manager?

She settled on a festive green blouse with black pants. She put on her black boots which gave her a little height and boosted her confidence. She put her arms on her hips and held her "power pose" before she left to catch the bus. Her professor in college had introduced their entire class to the benefits of doing a "power pose" before any important presentation.

Natalie's stomach began to do cartwheels as she pushed on the handle to the door to the conference room. She walked past the long table and put her black bag under the chair. She scooted the chair under the table. The mayor began the meeting by going over the agenda. Natalie noticed she was third on the list. When it came time for her to speak, she rose from her seat to the podium.

"Good morning, my name is Natalie Walker and I am here on behalf of Sandy Nelson. We are excited for the Festival of Trees Celebration next month. This event is held on December 22nd and has an average attendance of 2,500 people over the four hours of the event. We also have over 500 volunteers, from three years old to eighty."

Just as Natalie was about to finish up her presentation, the door opened.

"Sorry for the interruption. My last meeting ran long." Eli, dressed in a form-fitting gray suit, made his way to an empty seat right in front of Natalie. Man, he looked good in that suit. Their eyes met, staying connected for a few seconds. Natalie quickly looked down at her notes to find her place. She turned over her paper attempting to find where she left off.

"I umm, so yes the Festival and Live Nativity is scheduled for December 22nd."

Eli raised his left arm while holding his pen. Natalie nodded his way.

"If I recall, the numbers for this event have been declining in recent years," Eli said. "Can you tell us why?"

Natalie looked down at her notes, feeling her face becoming flushed. She took back her thought of thinking he looked handsome. Why was he always such a jerk about everything? Determined to not let Eli ruin this opportunity she gathered herself before responding, "Being on the 22nd of December means that we are competing with other events going on in the area as well as the typical holiday season. People are traveling for the holidays or are sick. We are hopeful with this year being our tenth year that we will bring some of those people back we've missed years prior. For many families, this event is a tradition, and we want to remind them why they come to it."

Eli looked down at his notes. "How is this year going to be different from years prior? If you're wanting to attract a bigger audience, I take it you've added some value to the festival, correct?"

Natalie tried to exhale as quietly as she could without going off on Eli and his condescending tone. Who did he think he was? Barely in Harbor Ridge for a month and already trying to talk about what the town did and didn't need, as if he was some expert on what people wanted.

"This year our theme is 'A Thrill of Hope.' We know that this past year has been difficult for many families in Harbor Ridge with the factory closing and businesses deciding to move to Roanoke. We are *hoping*, pun always intended . . ." Natalie laughed a little to herself. She looked around the room at stone-faced men in suits. She swallowed hard and continued, "We are hoping that this night can bring back some hope to Harbor Ridge. Since this is the tenth anniversary of the festival, we want to make it bigger than ever."

Eli looked up from his binder, "Have you thought about charging admission? I looked at the advertising budget for this event the city has already invested in and was surprised it was four thousand dollars. Seeing how the city is trying to recoup their losses, is this a possibility?" Eli set his pen next to his open binder that was covered in notes.

Natalie took a deep breath. Wow, this guy has no charitable bone in his body. "This festival is *supposed* to be a gift to the community. We will not be charging admission."

"For now." Eli interrupted. He looked around the conference table. "What effect does this festival have on the local economy? I'm not from around here, but do people travel to see this? Is there any revenue generated from this event?"

Natalie immediately spoke up. "To answer your first question. Yes, people travel for this event. This event is multi-generational, and we've had grandparents bring their grandchildren. Parents bring their children. Uncles bring their niece and nephew."

"From where?"

Natalie stared at Eli. Mrs. Nelson would have handled Eli's questions better. Natalie knew better than to make something up. "I can have that information for you tonight."

The room fell silent. *That's it. I've ruined the festival that Mrs. Nelson has always worked so hard for.*

"So can I count on your support?" Natalie finally asked.

"We will vote on the budget in two weeks," Eli said.

"Okay, thank you for your time."

She closed her notebook, pulled her purse over her shoulder, and left the boardroom. It wasn't the emphatic "yes" she'd been hoping for, but it certainly wasn't a "no", either. She hoped she hadn't let Sandy down. In years past, the Chamber had been enthusiastically behind the Festival and the Nativity. At least they had before Eli joined their team. His questions really irked her. She scowled. He had to make everything more difficult.

She stopped to look out the windows. Just in the two hours she had been in the building, snow had covered the ground, and it was still coming down. It clung to what few leaves were left in the trees and gave the bark a nice dusting.

"It's really coming down out there, but I guess you're used to it, right?"

Natalie looked up to see Eli grinning at her. If he hadn't just made her presentation more difficult, she'd even think he was adorable. Annoying, maybe, but adorable too.

"Yep, I am, but the city doesn't seem to be. The roads still haven't been salted near my apartment. The bus was sliding on the road here."

"You took the bus in this mess?"

"I didn't exactly have a choice. My car is still being worked on. They had to order a part."

Eli must have sensed her desperation. "Let me give you a ride home. I have four-wheel drive."

Natalie started to think of an excuse not to, but she was ready to go home.

"Thank you," she answered.

As they walked to the front door of city hall, Eli pushed it open. He then held out his arm to her. The bitterness she felt toward his abrupt questioning during their meeting melted away as her hands felt warm inside his.

He opened the passenger side car door and gently closed it back once she was inside.

He started the car to warm up.

Rubbing her hands together, Natalie sat in the passenger seat as Eli scraped the freshly fallen snow off the windshield. Then Eli got in and slowly drove out of the parking lot. There weren't many cars on the road. Most people had made the smart decision to stay put.

A large tree had fallen in the middle of Natalie's street, blocking entry to the parking garage. Bright orange cones were set up around the perimeter of a power truck. The building was dark.

"You can let me off here and I'll walk home," Natalie said.

"Don't be stubborn. It doesn't seem like you'll have power. You can stay with me until they get it turned back on," he said.

"Okay, if you insist," Natalie answered, secretly relieved to not have to return to her freezing townhouse with no groceries or heat.

Eli pulled his Tesla into the garage of his townhouse. They both got out of the car. As Eli opened the house door, he turned around to Natalie.

"I'm still getting settled, so things are kind of a mess."

They walked into his townhouse, and Natalie nearly tripped over a stack of books laying in the middle of the floor.

"You weren't joking around."

"I tried to warn you." Eli's eyes moved around the perimeter of the apartment. "Moving is such a pain." He shrugged. "I try to travel as a minimalist, but somehow, I still gathered all this stuff. I'm hoping to not collect as much stuff before my next assignment."

Natalie wandered around the apartment. Cardboard boxes sat half unpacked in the corner. Clothes were spilling out of a suitcase that was still folded.

"Would you like some help?"

Eli shrugged his shoulders. "That would be really nice of you."

"No problem. I like organizing things."

She looked around before settling on a box labeled "books." Easy enough. Eli went to the kitchen and brought back a pair of scissors. Natalie used them to open the box.

"What's your next assignment?" she asked as she put some of the books on the shelf.

"I won't know until after the new year. I work for a consulting firm that helps organizations redesign their structure to maximize returns."

"You mean how to help the company make more money? How to cut costs that aren't effective?"

Eli tilted his head to one side, "No not just making more money but also steering city leadership into capitalizing on their strengths."

Natalie shook her head. "There's more to life than money."

"It's hard to argue with numbers. For example, how much is the city spending on this little Festival of Trees celebration versus how much will the city make back? Those are the hard questions I have to ask."

Natalie's heart started beating faster. "*Little* Festival? For someone who's never been to it, you sure seem to think you know *everything* about it?"

"I did my research."

Natalie scoffed at the idea that he could possibly know more about her festival than she did in the few weeks he had moved to Harbor Ridge. "What research?"

Eli unpacked glasses from the moving box. "I read newspaper articles, watched the news clips of last year's event. Researched the hashtags on social media."

Natalie stopped unpacking a box of kitchen utensils and glared at him.

"But you haven't been to the Festival yourself. You haven't seen the lights on the trees or the ornaments and read the stories behind them. You haven't seen the children dressed for the Live Nativity or heard the high school choir sing the Christmas carols. It's magical. I love it."

The festival meant a great deal to Natalie. Three years ago, it had been what saved her from never wanting to celebrate Christmas again. New in Harbor Ridge, she went that night at Sandy's insistence as a volunteer. That night alone in the middle of the event surrounded by such peace and joy, it was though the sadness she had carried with her from her broken engagement was lifted. Now instead of thinking about December not being her wedding anniversary, she could focus on helping to put together the Festival of Trees and the Live Nativity.

Eli didn't know about any of that and she didn't plan to tell him. All he cared about was the festival's profits, not some personal testimony. She swallowed hard, diverting her thoughts back to the task at hand of helping Eli unpack.

Eli sensing the conversation getting heated changed the subject.

"So you mentioned you moved to Harbor Ridge three years ago. What brought you here? The job at the hospital?"

"I needed a change of scenery." That was putting it mildly.

"And did you find it?"

"Find what?"

"Whatever you were looking for?"

"Oh, I guess so. I love working at the hospital and sometimes subbing at the gym. Quinn and Luke are the sweetest kids. I've been helping my friend Sandy with the kids' Christmas musical at the church since it's right before choir practice and Quinn and Luke are so fun and energetic. They're adorable."

"They are pretty special kids. They're part of the reason I moved here. I wanted the chance to see them grow up, at least for a little while. I don't know how you do everything on your plate."

Natalie smiled as she looked down and opened a new box and removed the paper that had been protecting its contents.

"It all brings me joy, especially working with the kids."

She unwrapped a frame. She immediately recognized Eli first. He couldn't have been more than sixteen, and already a good-looking kid. Hannah looked so much like her mother. They both shared the same warm smile. There was another girl in the photo. At first Natalie dismissed her as maybe being a girlfriend or one of Hannah's friends, but she looked a little younger than the two of them. Eli noticed her looking at the frame and walked over. He took it from her and sighed.

"Those were some really great days, " he said as he put it back in the box.

Natalie reached out and rubbed his shoulder with her right hand. She reached back into the box and put the picture on the mantle above the fireplace. The fire was keeping them warm. Eli relented and let her put up the picture. He paused to admire it.

"Who is that girl in the picture?" Natalie asked quietly.

"That's our sister Amy," he said slowly and with a heaviness that made Natalie question why she had to ask such a personal question.

"Oh, I didn't know you had another sister. Hannah never mentioned her to me," she said, surprised. Then again, Natalie had never seen Amy in any of the pictures Hannah had at her house.

"I'm not surprised. Amy hasn't seen or spoken to either of us in four years. After our parents passed away, she was only seventeen and still had her senior year of high school left. Hannah really wanted to become Amy's legal guardian at least for that one year but Amy decided she wanted to move in with my aunt and uncle in California. They became her legal guardians until she turned eighteen. Amy ended up staying out in California to go to college."

"That's a long way from Harbor Ridge."

Eli nodded. "She should be graduating soon. I guess."

"You guess?"

Eli shrugged his shoulders. "Hannah tried to keep up with her and send her birthday cards and Christmas presents. Amy never responded to any of it so Hannah stopped trying. I tried finding out where she was and what she was doing but I didn't have any luck. I don't want to put my aunt and uncle in the middle so I don't ask them any questions. Amy is an adult now, if she doesn't want to be a part of our family anymore that's up to her." Eli said with a hint of sadness.

"I'm sorry."

"Me too. I feel the worst for Hannah. Her and Amy were really close and I know Hannah feels betrayed." He glanced up again at the picture. "We all lost so much." He ran his fingers through his hair and sighed.

Natalie pulled out another picture frame from the box. In it was a teenage Eli with frosted blond hair wearing a black tuxedo with a bright orange vest, the same color as his date's dress. Very orange.

"Tell me you went to high school in the early 2000s, without telling me you went to high school in the early 2000s." Natalie couldn't contain her laughter.

He grabbed the frame from her hands.

"And the sad part is, I thought I looked good."

"You did look good." Natalie caught herself. "For a wannabe boy band member, I suppose."

"Oh, ouch." Eli mimicked getting stabbed through the heart and playfully took the frame back from Natalie and laughed. "I'd like to know what teenage Natalie wore to her prom?"

"Oh no. There will be no photo evidence of that shared."

"I bet you looked beautiful." He smiled at Natalie.

Natalie found herself smiling back at him.

They spent the remainder of the afternoon unpacking the boxes. Each box seemed to tell a story. Eli kept a coffee mug or a picture frame from each of the cities he had lived in the past six years. He opened a box that contained old CDs. They discovered they both liked *Jimmy Eat World*. It was the soundtrack of their youth.

Natalie looked at her phone. "It's four o'clock?"

They had been unpacking for five hours.

"It can't be. I'm sorry I kept you here so late."

"It was no problem at all. I had the day off."

Natalie caught herself smiling. She wished she could have stayed hours longer. There was something about Eli that drew her in. She didn't have to try hard to make conversation. It was effortless. The way it should be. Even still, she couldn't let herself go there. Starting a new romance scared her. It shouldn't with how much time had passed, but she had been hurt before by who she trusted most.

"Thanks for all your help today unpacking."

"No problem. It was fun. I like organizing things."

He smiled back at her. "Well feel free to come back anytime and do more of that."

Eli dropped her off at her apartment later that afternoon after she got an email from the electric company that power had been restored. As she turned her key to get in the door she turned and was surprised to see Eli still in his car watching her safely enter her apartment. She waved goodbye to him and smiled. It felt nice to have someone looking out for her.

Chapter Ten

A small mountain of freshly washed clothes sat atop Ben and Hannah's bed. The washing and drying was the easy part. The folding and putting away, well, that always took twice as long.

"Ready to go?" Ben asked.

Hannah, dressed in leggings and one of Ben's old college sweatshirts, stepped out of their walk-in closet with a defeated look on her face.

"Are you sure we should leave the kids?"

"Yes," Ben said as he walked toward her. He embraced her before spinning her around kissing her.

"No kids for the whole weekend? We're going."

"So if the kids aren't going to come with us, are your laptop and cell phone staying home too?"

Hannah could see she pushed a button.

Ben crossed his arm and sat down on the bed next to her.

"Hannah, we've been through this. It's only for emergencies. I have to be reachable at all times. You get called into work at the hospital sometimes when you're supposed to be off."

Hannah stood up from the bed and walked to the corner of their room. Just like him to make this about her than admit he had a problem disconnecting from his cell phone. It might as well be attached.

"What's the point of having vacation time if you don't even use it fully?" Her voice rising with every word.

Ben remained sitting on the bed. "Why are we starting out our trip on such a sour note? It's like you've already decided you don't want to have a good time?"

Hannah scoffed at the assumption. She couldn't remember the last time she had been on vacation. "I want to have a good time, I just don't want to be second in your life."

Ben walked over to her and put his arms around her. Hannah kept her arms by her side. "That's not fair. You're not second."

She pulled back. "Well I'm certainly not your first priority."

"I want to go on this trip. I thought you did too. Why are you picking a fight right before we leave?" His voice stayed steady. He was always the calm amidst the chaos.

"You're right. We can talk about this later. I'll finish packing and get dressed," she said as she put another outfit on her side of the suitcase, taking up the only space on the bed not occupied by the laundry.

Natalie arrived five minutes before they were expecting her, early as usual. She appreciated Natalie's attentiveness and felt better about leaving her kids in Natalie's capable hands. Even so, Hannah spent the last few minutes before Natalie arrived writing the three pages of notes she planned to leave.

"Now remember we're just a few hours away so if you need us for any reason . . ."

"I'll call. I promise," Natalie assured her.

"We keep an extra phone in the cabinet above the microwave in case the kids go to separate places and they need a way to contact us. The phone can only call or text certain numbers and doesn't have internet. I like having them be able to contact me if necessary, so feel free to send it with Luke or Quinn tomorrow. And the kids' pediatrician's number, the poison center, Eli's number . . ."

"Are all on the fridge, you told me." Natalie interjected with a smile. "Go, have a great time. The kids and I are going to have fun this weekend. You should too."

Hannah gave Natalie a hug. She was worried for nothing. The kids were going to have the best time hanging out with Natalie. "Thank you so much! I left money for pizza for dinner tonight and extra spending money on the counter beside my car and house key if you need it."

Ben rolled their suitcase into the kitchen. "Honey, it's time to go." The tone of his voice still held some hurt. Hannah felt guilty for bringing the cell phone thing up right before they left.

"I'm coming, I'm coming." They gave the kids one last long hug each.

They walked out to the driveway in silence. Hannah quietly slipped into the passenger side and closed the door. She heard the suitcase thud into the trunk and then Ben sat down in the driver's seat. Ben reached across the console and squeezed her hand. And they started their trip just like every family trip. With a prayer.

"God, please give us a safe trip on the road today and when we return. Be with Quinn and Luke and especially Natalie this weekend."

"Yes, Lord." Hannah added with a smile, knowing full well what it took to have the kids full time.

"Thank you for the gift of being able to get away. Let it be a blessing for our marriage and for our family. Amen."

"Amen."

She turned and smiled at him. She knew she was exactly where she needed to be.

"Do you need anything before we head out?" Ben asked.

Just one thing, she thought to herself. She unbuckled her seatbelt and kissed him like she hadn't in years.

"Much more of that this weekend, I'm hoping?"

Hannah smiled.

"Oh yeah. More of that."

* * *

Natalie pushed the silver button on the coffee machine a fourth time and watched in vain as nothing came down into her mug.

Despite it being the kids' first time with their parents away, they'd stayed in their beds the whole night. It was Natalie who'd had a difficult time going to sleep. She'd heard weird noises all night long and tossed and turned before dozing off after two a.m.

She'd been woken up at 6:30 by a ding from her phone: a text message notification. The mom who was supposed to take Luke to his soccer game was sick and couldn't do it. Luke needed to be at the gym at 9 a.m. The exact time Quinn needed to be at her ballet lesson across town.

Natalie began to panic. What was she going to do? She didn't want to bother Hannah so early on her trip.

After spending twenty minutes trying to figure out how to work their coffee machine, she finally gave up. The sun was peeking through the blinds in the kitchen. Natalie looked up and noticed Luke and Quinn had come down to the kitchen. Natalie explained their predicament and asked if they had another family friend who may be able to help them.

"Call Uncle Eli. He can help us," Luke said.

Natalie sighed, not who she meant.

"No, I can figure this out. We don't need to bother your uncle." Natalie answered in between a yawn.

"It's ringing." Quinn answered as she handed the phone to Natalie.

In a haste, Natalie pressed end on the phone.

"Where did you get a cell phone?" Natalie asked, knowing Hannah's stance.

Quinn raised her shoulders up and then let them fall. "Mom left it for us. In case of an emergency."

Natalie then remembered Hannah showing her where it was before she left. Natalie looked down at Quinn's eager expression and shook her head. "This is not an emergency."

Natalie put the phone back on the counter and exhaled. She hoped the call didn't go through to Eli. He'd probably have something to say about her not being able to handle the kids. She didn't want to bother him on his day off. Relieved he didn't pick up, she turned back to Luke and Quinn. "Who wants to play?"

Just then the phone on the counter buzzed. Natalie reached for it over Quinn. She sighed as she saw the name on the call.

"Hello?" Natalie answered.

"Who is this?" an agitated voice answered the other side.

"Hi Eli. It's Natalie. I'm staying over with the kids this weekend while Ben and Hannah are out of town. Quinn thought it would be funny to give you a call so early."

Quinn smiled a mischievous smile revealing a missing front tooth.

"In over your head already?" Eli yawned.

Natalie put her left hand on her hip. "As a matter of fact, we are doing just fine. Thank you."

"Really, so you wouldn't mind if I talked to the kids?" Eli asked.

Natalie took her time responding to his question, "Well we might have a slight scheduling problem."

"I'm on my way," Eli answered.

* * *

Eli softly knocked on the front door with his spare right hand. His left hand held a drink tray with two hot coffees and muffins from the coffee shop across from his townhouse.

Natalie opened the door and he could immediately tell she must not have gotten much sleep. Her hair was pulled up on the top of her head and her eyes were glazed over. She still managed to look cute. Somehow. Quinn peeked out from behind Natalie's back.

"Uncle Eli!"

He set the coffees and bag on the side table just inside the door. Quinn ran up to him with her arms open. Quinn gave the best hugs. His little niece exuded happiness and he was glad he could spend time with her. As soon as he stood up, Quinn ran back to the kitchen.

"Thank you for coming." Natalie eyed the two drinks in his hand. "And for bringing caffeine. Have you tried to work their coffee pot before? Mine is pretty straightforward—just press *on*."

"Oh you think this is for you? It is early."

"Oh I understand." The hope in Natalie's eyes turned to disappointment.

Eli grabbed one out of the gray container holding them. He smiled "I'm just kidding. Of course one is for you. You don't think I'm that terrible of a person?"

Natalie blew on the coffee before taking a sip. "Well now that you mention it."

Eli smirked. "I see then."

"This definitely redeems you a little in my book." Natalie smiled and scrunched up her nose. He loved when she did that. Her laugh was infectious and made him forget it was seven forty-five a.m. on a Saturday when he could be doing anything. There was truthfully nowhere he'd rather be than with his niece and nephew. He was starting to feel the same way about being with Natalie. There was something about her demeanor that made him feel excited to be around her. He loved giving her a hard time. Loved even more she could dish it back.

Eli agreed to take Luke to his soccer game. Natalie would bring Quinn back to meet them when her dance class was finished. Eli stood toward the back of the bleachers as he watched Luke play. He was looking forward to Natalie and Quinn joining him. He hadn't met many of the other families and small talk was not his favorite activity. He noticed Natalie and Quinn entering through the gym door. He waved at them and Natalie smiled and waved back as they made their way to him.

Quinn sat down in between Eli and Natalie. Eli eyed the brown bag Natalie had set on the floor in front of them.

"Quinn told me that Hannah usually packs lunches for everyone to eat so we picked some sandwiches up on our way," Natalie smiled.

Eli nodded. "Those look delicious. I'm starving."

Quinn pulled on his shirt. "Uncle Eli, can I please go play with my friends?" She looked over at a group of girls at the lower part of the bleachers.

He nodded. "Sure thing."

"Just make sure you can always see us and we can see you," Natalie added.

Natalie scooted closer to Eli as she reached down for the bag of sandwiches.

"Yeah Luke!" Eli cheered as Luke made a goal. He looked over and as his eyes met Natalie's, she smiled and set her sandwich on her lap and clapped her hands cheering him on.

"So did you play soccer growing up too?" Natalie asked this question right as Eli took a huge bite of his BLT. He held up his finger as he finished chewing.

"I'm sorry. Take your time."

Eli swallowed. "I played club soccer. Those were some great years." He looked back down at the indoor field Luke and the boys were playing on and found himself thinking back to growing up playing ball. His parents always cheering him on. Now it was a joy to get to do that for Luke too. He wished his parents could have been there.

"And you?" he looked over to Natalie. "What did you like doing growing up?"

"I was on the dance team. I had tried out for cheerleading and didn't make it. But the joke was on them because I ended up liking the dance team even more than cheerleading. Plus I also had time to join the choir too, which I wouldn't have been able to do if I was on the cheer squad."

"Do you still dance?"

Natalie laughed. "Does step aerobics count?"

Eli shook his head. "I don't think so. What about singing?"

"I still sing sometimes. I'm singing tomorrow at church for the Christmas cantata."

Quinn walked back over to the two of them. "Natalie, I'm still hungry."

* * *

Natalie took Quinn to the concession stand to get a snack.

"I haven't seen you at a game before. Which kid is yours?" the cashier asked Natalie.

Natalie pointed Luke out on the field.

"Your son looks so much like your husband," the cashier said.

Natalie turned beet red.

"Oh he's not my husband. He's their uncle and I'm just the babysitter. Their parents are out of town this weekend," she answered.

"Wow, those family genes must be strong then."

Natalie was hoping the redness in her face would go away before she got back to the bleachers.

It was a long afternoon after the kids' activities and traffic was heavy on their way back. Well as heavy as it got in Harbor Ridge. Natalie was relieved when Eli offered to stay over for dinner and help, especially considering the kids both had important school projects due on Monday. Natalie was once again unsure of how she could be in two places at once. How could she help both Quinn and Luke at the same time with two very different projects? Natalie knew Hannah was a rockstar nurse, but she had even greater respect for how Hannah managed her household. It wasn't easy, that was for sure. This must've been why they said it takes a village to raise a family.

Eli helped Luke with his science project while Natalie helped Quinn with her show and tell project. Quinn's assignment was to fill a paper bag with five items from her house that told the class about her favorite things about Christmas. Naturally Eli had selected helping Luke with his model of the solar system. "Anything but more Christmas," Eli mumbled.

Natalie sat down with Quinn on the cozy rug in the living room to brainstorm some ideas on what to include in her bag.

Quinn started biting her fingernails. "This is hard. How am I supposed to narrow it down to just five things? What do you love about Christmas?"

"All of it. I can't do your assignment for you, but if I were doing it, I'd say I would include a candy cane because I love peppermint. A songbook because of all the beautiful music. Maybe a special ornament? What are your favorite things about Christmas?"

Quinn's eyes widened as she looked in the corner of the room where the family's Christmas tree stood. It was fake because Luke was allergic but the tree more than made up for it in size and stature.

It was a seven-and-a-half-foot tree carefully decorated with breakable ornaments on the higher branches and kid friendly ones at the bottom. Hannah had let Natalie in on that little secret when she had come over for coffee one morning. Natalie made sure to tuck away that little trick for when she had kids, if she ever did. The topper was an angel that had belonged to her grandparents. Hannah had pointed it out to Natalie the first time they had put it up. Hannah's grandmother had sewn the angel together and the lace for the angel's wings had come from a part of her wedding dress.

Quinn stood up and walked over to the tree, her hazel eyes followed it from top to bottom. She turned back to Natalie. "I love the Christmas lights. When it gets dark at night and I walk up the stairs to my bedroom, the last thing I see are the lights. And in the morning when I wake up and walk downstairs, the lights are the first thing I see in the morning."

"That is a perfect start! I'm going to check on your brother and see how his solar system is coming along. I'll be right back."

Natalie walked into the dining room to find Eli and Luke sitting opposite each other at the kitchen table surrounded by different sizes of white styrofoam balls and paint supplies. There must have been at least a dozen of them and some had rolled off under the table and across the room. Two jars of paint sat opened and a little too close to the edge. The table looked similar to Eli's townhouse—a complete disaster. Natalie began to stress out. She liked to keep things neat and organized.

She grabbed that day's newspaper from the counter and started unfolding it. She walked over to where Eli and Luke were sitting.

"We should put the newspaper down while you're both painting. I don't want the paint to ruin the furniture."

Eli continued painting a giant white styrofoam ball red. Without looking up he said, "Relax, we've got it under control. And plus it's washable paint. I know what I'm doing."

Natalie was not convinced and started moving the paint to make room for the newspaper to go on the table.

As she reached across Eli to put the newspaper underneath the planet, Eli stuck the tip of his paintbrush in the red paint before putting it on the edge of Natalie's nose.

"Calm down, Rudolph."

The paint felt cold on Natalie's nose and her head jerked back. Luke giggled as Eli smirked before going back to their project. Natalie put one hand on her hip before walking back to the kitchen sink. She grabbed a paper towel to wipe the red paint off her nose. Eli stood up from the table and walked over to her. Natalie poked him in the shoulder.

"You know, I'm going to have to charge your sister for an extra child if you don't watch it."

"Oh come on, I was just joking around. Besides, I know how much you love Santa and his reindeer. You'd fit right in." He let out a smile. She couldn't help but smile at him. Why did he have to look so adorable when he was misbehaving?

"I do. Doesn't mean I want to be one though. Did I get it all off?"

Eli tore off a piece of paper towel. He moved closer to her gently wiping the extra red paint off her nose. Natalie looked into his playful eyes. His five o'clock shadow illuminated under the kitchen lighting. He'd never looked more handsome.

Luke wandered in the kitchen after Eli. "I'm hungry. What's for dinner?"

Eli took a step back from Natalie before adding "Yeah, what's for dinner?"

Natalie bent down to Luke's level. "I don't know. What should Uncle Eli make us?"

She turned to Eli with a half smile on her face.

"Mac and cheese. Mac and cheese!" Luke yelled out.

Natalie walked to the pantry and picked up a box of instant Mac and cheese. She brought it back to the kitchen island. Eli picked up the box with two fingers and held it as far away from him as he could. "What is this?"

Natalie rolled her eyes. "Dinner."

"You've never made mac and cheese from scratch?" he asked in disbelief.

Natalie lifted her shoulders in a shrug. "I can't say I have."

Eli opened the kitchen cabinet next to the oven. He shuffled around a few pots and then pulled out a silver stockpot. He lifted it and set it on the back burner. Eli turned back to Natalie with a smile that showed off his dimples. "You are in for a big treat." He motioned to Luke's project. "You go help Luke and Quinn with their projects and I'll make dinner. Deal?"

"Whatever you say," Natalie muttered.

As Natalie walked back to the table, Eli hollered. "Make sure you keep the paint off the table though. Wouldn't want to ruin the furniture."

Natalie rolled her eyes back at him as he winked at her. As hard as she tried to fight it, a smile came across her face. She sat down at the table as Luke got back to work painting the solar system. She lifted another paintbrush. Out of the corner of her eye, she watched Eli fill the pan with tap water before setting it on the stove. She would have watched him for longer except a little voice interrupted her. "Look what I found!"

Quinn sat down next to Natalie with her full bag of Christmas treasures, her eyes glittering with excitement. Natalie couldn't help but absorb some of her enthusiasm. She rested her chin on her fist, "What did you put in your special bag?"

Quinn poured out the contents of her brown paper sack on the table in front of them. Very delicately, as if it was her most prized possession, Quinn picked up a small silver bell attached to a red string.

"I found this bell." Quinn held up it and shook it. She pulled out a piece of foil wrapped candy next.

"A chocolate candy, because who doesn't like chocolate?"

"I agree!"

Quinn began unraveling the foil paper. "They're my mom's favorite. She said they were her mom's favorite too. They have peanut butter in them."

"Maybe we should wait until after dinner. What do you have next?"

Quinn forgot all about the piece of chocolate candy and moved on to the next item on the table.

"The Christmas lights. I love the colored lights we put on the tree and the white lights we put outside."

"Fantastic choice. I will get a few replacement bulbs that will fit in your bag." Natalie paused and looked at the Christmas tree shining brightly in the corner of the room. She loved the decorations and special personalized ornaments. It told the story of their family. One day Natalie hoped she could have a special tree like that. Her parents kept one when she was a kid. It held ornaments from all the special trips they took, handmade ornaments she and her brother had made in school. Someday, maybe she'd have children whose ornaments she could put on a tree. She dismissed the thought and went back to helping Luke finish painting Jupiter to complete his solar system.

As Luke put the finishing coat on the last planet, Eli yelled from the kitchen. "Dinner is ready."

Natalie set the table and got everyone's drinks while Eli plated the mac and cheese.

The kids immediately dug in once the mac and cheese cooled slightly. Natalie stuck her fork in it before taking a bite. She sensed Eli watching her as she slowly took a second bite.

"Wow, this is delicious," she said as she took another bite.

Eli smiled smugly, "See I told you it was so much better than from a box."

Natalie nodded. "You'll have to show me the recipe and how to make it."

"I didn't follow a recipe. I just tasted as I went along," he said in between bites of mac and cheese. "I've made this enough that I don't need the recipe. Besides, I change it up quite a bit as well depending on who I'm cooking for and when."

Natalie wondered if he had been cooking for anyone special lately. She took another bite, "It is delicious and creamy. I look forward to trying your other kinds some time."

He smiled as he looked across the table. "I'd like that too." Natalie didn't need the mac and cheese to warm her up anymore.

They divided and conquered the bedtime routine. Natalie read stories to Quinn, while Eli read to Luke. After getting Quinn to bed, Natalie started cleaning the kitchen. She rinsed the dishes leftover from their dinner and started to put them in the dishwasher.

She heard footsteps coming down the stairs. Eli emerged from the stairwell.

"Luke finally went to sleep. He's a chatterbox."

"They were both exhausted." Natalie yawned. "I am too. I don't know how Hannah does it."

She resumed washing the remaining bowls and cups in the sink. Eli walked over to the sink and stood side by side to Natalie.

"They're never going to get clean if you don't rinse them off first."

And Eli was back to being Eli.

Natalie rubbed the side of her head. The long day getting to her. "Is it possible for you to not comment on everything you notice?"

He walked up beside her about to take a bowl from the dishwasher to rewash.

Natalie turned the water off and picked up the faucet sprayer. She held the spray nozzle in Eli's direction. Eli took two steps back as he put his hands up.

Natalie waved the nozzle at him. "Back away from the sink. I'm going to do the dishes and you're going to sit quietly while I finish."

Eli reached for a dish in the sink. Weeks of aggravation came to a head as Natalie pushed the button spraying cold water all over Eli's chest, splashing up in his face.

His shoulders tensed up as he shivered, his face a mix of shock and disbelief. He lifted his shirt to wipe the droplets of water running down his neck.

Natalie bit her lip to keep from laughing.

"Wow, I didn't think you had that in you."

A trail of water droplets followed after Eli as he walked up the stairs in silence. Natalie wasn't sure if he was going to come back or not and she welcomed some peace and quiet after going nonstop all day. He had been bugging her for weeks over the festival, her job, and now the dishes. He thought he knew everything about everything. Natalie let out a sigh as she looked at the dishes still on the stove. *Gah*, his mac and cheese was delicious though, some of the best she had ever tasted. Why did he have to be so smug about it? First, she wiped up the floor and then she conquered the stovetop dishes. It was a small price to pay for the best mac and cheese she had ever eaten.

Eli walked downstairs with a new shirt on and his hair combed to the side, still wet from Natalie spraying him with water. She briefly thought about apologizing but he deserved it after the way he'd been treating her. Besides, it was just water.

"Is it safe now?" Eli asked.

Natalie put her left hand on her hip, "Depends. Are you still going to act like a know-it-all?"

"It's not my fault I happen to know a lot about various topics. I was just trying to be helpful."

"Mansplaining is more like it."

He folded his arms, "How incredibly sexist of you. You've never heard of woman-splaining?"

Natalie rolled her eyes and put her hand on her hip. She nodded toward the dishwasher. "I happen to know how to wash dishes too, you know."

"Fine, do it your way. I'll save my 'told you so' speech when you have to run the dishwasher a second time."

"We will see about that."

Eli sat down on the couch, propped his feet on the coffee table, and pulled out his phone.

"What are you doing? Playing a game? Or on a dating app?" Natalie squeezed out that last comment. She figured a guy like him must be constantly going on dates. He was charming, sometimes, and had a great job.

Eli looked up and laughed. "No, definitely not. I'm doing work, trying to answer some emails that keep piling up. There are some developers that want to bring their businesses to Harbor Ridge, but have some questions about long-term viability."

"I see. So what do you tell them?"

"I show them the graphs and statistics about the number of restaurants and businesses that come to town and are successful after a year."

"Do you think the developers want to come?"

"Some do, sure." He sighed. "I'm not sure it's the smartest business decision on their end. Harbor Ridge is struggling to maintain the residents it has now. If they come, they may not have many customers."

Natalie wiped down the kitchen table. Eli stood up from the couch and grabbed a paper towel from the counter and wiped down the opposite side of the table. She liked how he was attentive enough to notice she was working hard to clean up. Maybe he wasn't completely oblivious.

"Thanks for helping me finish cleaning the kitchen."

Eli held his hand out for Natalie to give him her worn paper towel. He threw them both away in the trash can. Then Natalie walked over to the couch with Eli close behind.

"No problem. Many hands make light work."

"They sure do. I am feeling tired from today. Way more tired than I ever did from a job working at my desk."

Eli nodded in agreement. "The kids can be exhausting, that's for sure."

"I'm glad they're in bed and finally asleep. I've been wanting to watch a movie all month and it premieres tonight."

Eli rolled his eyes. "Please don't tell me it's one of those awful Christmas movies?"

Of course. Why would he like anything cheery or hopeful or festive? *He's like a real-life Grinch.*

"You don't have to watch it," Natalie reassured him.

Eli nodded, "So it *is* one of those awful movies."

Natalie shook her head. There was nothing wrong with her wanting a little low-key Christmas escape. As much as she loved the holidays, her obligations to Hannah, the church and her job were taking their toll. Especially after the busy weekend they had, she needed a chance to watch something effortless. Besides, what did Eli know? They were cute movies.

Natalie pulled the white blanket from the recliner close by and covered her lower half with the fuzzy white blanket.

Eli stood up and walked over to the fireplace. "Do you mind if I get a fire going?"

She nodded, "That sounds nice. Although you'll have to show me how to put it out before you leave."

"I was going to stay the night if that's okay with you? I promised Luke I would make breakfast in the morning. He loves my French toast. Usually I just make it when they visit but that hasn't been too often. I can stay on the couch."

"Sure that sounds fine."

Natalie thought it was sweet he wanted to do that for Luke. Now she didn't have to worry about weird noises if Eli was around. He would be the first to be found.

She diverted her attention back to the television above the fireplace. The cackling of burning firewood provided the perfect setting for this week's Christmas movie.

Eli came over with two bowls of ice cream and sat at the opposite corner of the couch. The movie began.

On screen the two characters bumped into each other outside of a cafe. He spilled his coffee on her white sweater.

Eli whispered, "They're going to end up together."

"Shhh," Natalie swatted at him. She pulled back her hand but it was too late. Eli's bowl slid out of his hands and the chocolate ice cream landed on the beige couch.

Natalie jumped up from the couch. "Oh no. Oh no. Oh no." Natalie's eyes grew larger by the second as the ice cream melted into the couch.

Eli shrugged. "Relax. You are wound way too tight. It's just a couch."

Eli went back to the kitchen to grab some stain remover under the sink and a clean rag. He gently sprayed the spot and then blotted it away.

"See? Better than before."

Eli was right: the stain was gone. Not a mark left in sight. It was too bad life wasn't like that. Hurts couldn't just be sprayed away leaving no trace.

Eli went back into the kitchen to get more ice cream. They ate it at the kitchen table. Natalie did not want a repeat of spilling anything on the couch.

"I don't think I thanked you for coming over this morning and helping me with the kids. I couldn't have done it without you. They adore you." It was not hard to see why. He gave up his entire Saturday to be with them. To help her out. Sure, he had his annoying qualities, but she was beginning to see another side to Eli. A genuine, kind side and a delicious cook.

He scratched his eyebrow, "They're great kids. So funny. They take after their uncle. But they're way smarter than I was at their age."

"Obviously," Natalie's lips curled up as she licked the spoon. "They're lucky you get to be with them."

"For now," Eli looked down at his bowl as he took another bite.

"When do you think . . ." she paused. She wanted to ask him when he thought he'd hear about his next assignment. But that seemed pushy, and why would he want to tell her, anyway? They weren't an item. They were barely even friends. Every time she started to like him, he gave her another reason not to.

"When do I think *what*?" Eli asked.

"Hannah and Ben will get back tomorrow?" Natalie asked, thinking quickly on her feet.

"After lunch I believe."

Cheery music began playing. Natalie turned to see the two main characters of the movie sharing a kiss under the mistletoe.

"Oh no, I'm missing the movie." Natalie stuck out her bottom lip pretending to pout.

"Who would have guessed how they would end up?" As he smiled at her, Natalie could feel her cheeks getting warm.

She kept fighting the feelings she had for Eli but they were getting harder and harder to ignore. How could he drive her absolutely nuts one moment, and then sit on the couch next to her acting all dreamy and chivalrous? Still, she had to push the feelings away. As soon as she felt any kind of excitement or romance all she could do was flashback to four years ago. The weeks she spent crying. The dreams she had for her future were erased. Her family had encouraged her to start dating again. So had her friends. Rachel had even offered to help set up a dating profile on one of the dating apps but Natalie wasn't ready yet.

There was too much to risk. Life was good enough now. Predictable. Safe. Where would she even start? Say her and Eli started dating and things went south. Then what would come of her relationship with Hannah? Or her relationship with the kids? Not to mention Eli didn't seem interested in the least, and Natalie wasn't sure she was, either . . .even if today had been some of the most fun she'd had in a while.

"What are you thinking about?" Eli's question broke her train of thought.

"Nothing." She stood up from the table. "I'm ready for bed. I've got an early morning tomorrow."

* * *

Eli was sad to see Natalie go to bed. He enjoyed spending time with her and talking about traveling and books they enjoyed. She must be an early riser and he was a night owl. Yet another way that they were opposites. Eli pulled out his laptop from the bag he'd left near the sofa. It would be easier to respond to email on his laptop instead of his phone. One of the emails he received was from a town in Colorado asking for his references for a job that started in the middle of January.

He put his ice cream bowl in the sink and rinsed it out before going back to work.

Chapter Eleven

Natalie came downstairs to the kitchen the next morning, having slept much better than the night before. She woke up early to get dressed for the Christmas musical at church. She wore black slacks and a red button-down blouse and had blown out her hair and applied more than her usual amount of makeup. The choir was singing their special Christmas cantata and Natalie was singing the solo in "O Holy Night."

She was surprised to see the kids and Eli already up at the kitchen table. A stack of French toast sat in the middle of the table. Luke was too busy eating to notice Natalie in the kitchen. Quinn stood up from her chair at the table to give Natalie a hug.

"You look so pretty, Natalie."

Eli immediately started running his fingers through his hair trying to flatten the rogue piece of hair that was standing straight up.

"Thanks, today is our Christmas cantata," she answered.

"I want to go," Quinn said.

Natalie looked at the clock on the stove. "I need to leave in fifteen minutes. If you can both be ready I'll take you with me."

Luke and Quinn stood up from their chairs so fast they nearly knocked over their juice cups.

Eli laughed, "I've never seen them so excited about something before."

"They have donuts after the service, if they haven't gotten enough of a sugar high with the syrup." Natalie joked. She grabbed the empty coffee mug and put it in the sink.

"Wait, don't turn that on," Eli leaped from his chair at the kitchen table.

It was too late. She turned on the faucet and let out a yelp.

The freezing water startled her. The water sprayed toward her instead of down into the sink, soaking her face and her perfectly ironed red blouse. She wiped the water dripping down her face and smeared black mascara under her eyes.

Natalie turned to him with water dripping from her hair to the floor. Just when she thought she had Eli all figured out.

Eli's eyes widened in disbelief as he tried to explain what just happened. "I didn't mean . . . I put a piece of tape under the faucet after I made breakfast. It was supposed to be a joke. I forgot you'd be all dressed up for your cantata. I thought you'd be in pajamas or whatever."

Natalie squeezed her hair into a paper towel as she tried to dry her hair. "Why would you do that?"

"It was just supposed to be a joke," he repeated. "To get back at you for soaking me last night."

"Yeah because, last night, you were being a jerk." She wiped the water off her forehead before refocusing her gaze on him, her voice raised, "For the last few weeks, you've been a jerk. I don't have anything else to wear. And my hair." She pulled it close to her face before releasing it in disgust, "I spent half an hour on it. You really are the worst!"

He rushed over to her and grabbed some paper towels. He laid them down on the floor to soak up the water dripping off the counter making a puddle. Natalie tried helplessly to blot her blouse, but it was no use. Eli tried helping fix Natalie's hair. Exacerbated, Natalie threw the roll of paper towels at him. Eli caught the roll and smiled which aggravated Natalie even more.

"What can I do to help?" Eli asked as a peace offering.

At that moment Quinn, wearing a green velvet dress with white tights, and Luke, wearing navy dress pants and a button down white shirt, bounced down the stairs.

"We're ready to go!" Luke announced.

Quinn looked confused at Natalie. "What happened to you?"

Natalie looked at the well-dressed kids, to Eli still in his plaid pajamas and t-shirt, and then back to the kids.

She pointed her finger at Eli. "This is his fault."

"That wasn't nice of him." Quinn stated, giving Eli a dirty look.

"No it wasn't." She looked over at Eli who immediately put his hands up.

"Hey now. You were the one spraying water on me last night."

Quinn's mouth opened wide as she gasped. "Natalie? Is that true?"

Natalie stared down Eli. "Well yes technically but only after he put red paint on my face and he was being a total jerk."

"Mom and Dad don't like it when we fight or name-call," Luke said. "They usually send us to our rooms to think about what we've done."

"And make us apologize and hug," Quinn added disapprovingly.

Natalie tucked her hair behind her right ear and bent down to Quinn's eye level. "Sweetie, I've got to get to my choir concert. I can't go to my room. Besides, I don't live here."

"Fine. But you and Uncle Eli can at least hug and say you're sorry." Quinn turned to look at Eli who was standing in the corner of the kitchen, doing his best to not crack up at how serious Quinn's tone was. It was clear she had gotten this lecture from Hannah a time or two.

Natalie stood up and crossed her arms. Eli walked over and opened his arms to give Natalie a hug while Natalie kept her arms crossed.

Quinn shook her head. "Like you mean it, Natalie."

Eli wiped a smudge of black mascara off Natalie's cheek with his thumb. He spoke softly into her ear. "I am sorry. Being around the kids reminds me so much of when Hannah and I were little. I didn't mean to mess up your outfit. You looked beautiful."

He pulled away from her. Natalie let a smile come over her face for the first time that morning.

"I'm sorry too. I shouldn't have sprayed you with water last night. I was just tired."

She pulled him close and hugged him back. She felt safe in his arms. He rubbed her back as she rested her head on his shoulder. A few moments passed as it seemed like they were the only two in the kitchen. She didn't want to let go until she saw the clock on the microwave and suddenly, Natalie pulled back. "You're going to have to take the kids to church."

"What?"

"You asked what you could do to help me and this is it. Take them to church for me so I can dry my blouse and fix my hair and make-up."

Eli was uncertain about this new plan. "What *else* can I do to help?"

"Haven't you done enough already? I've got to go before I'm late."

Natalie jumped into her car to get to practice on time. She left Eli and the kids behind to figure out what to do. She was nervous enough as it was, and then Eli had to go and ruin her morning.

The kids were going to be so disappointed if they missed out on the cantata. She barely made it into her seat before the director tapped his baton on his music stand for the choir to stand up and begin their rehearsal. The choir had a short break before the cantata began and Natalie went to get a drink from the water fountain. She had been in such a hurry to leave that she left her water and coffee on the kitchen counter. Her throat was dry, but she knew it was just nerves. She made her way back to her seat on the end of the row. The orchestra began playing "Carol of the Bells."

Soon it was time for "O Holy Night." Her solo was at the beginning. As she stood up to the microphone she thought about how much the song meant to her.

A thrill of hope the weary world rejoices.

As she finished her solo and the congregation applauded. Her eyes traced the crowd as she saw familiar friends. Tucked in the very last row on the end of the pew, she noticed Eli, with a surprised look on his face clapping. Their eyes met but she quickly looked away.

She couldn't keep the smile from spreading on her face as she headed back to her seat. She was glad she didn't see him before she started her solo or she may have been too nervous to even start singing.

As she left the choir loft she walked to the donut room passing several people on her way. Sandy came up and gave her a hug.

"Wow Natalie! Your solo was exquisite. So beautiful. It brought tears to my eyes. "O Holy Night" is my favorite Christmas carol."

"Thank you. It's mine too." Natalie smiled.

"Are you still available to meet tomorrow to go over the Festival of Trees event coming up?"

"Of course, I'm looking forward to it."

"Great." Sandy left juggling her warm cup of coffee with her bag.

Natalie reached out for a donut and as she turned around was face to face with Eli.

"You made it. I must say I'm surprised."

Eli reached behind her, grabbed a donut, and took a bite. "These are delicious." He took another bite. "The kids are hard to say no to. Good thing I'm not a parent. Yet. I didn't know you could sing like that. I mean, "O Holy Night" is overplayed, like most Christmas songs, but you sang it well."

His out-of-control bedhead was now combed down, and he had traded his pajamas for gray slacks and a light blue sweater. The aroma of his aftershave and the smell of the sugary donuts in the air tickled Natalie's nose.

"Thank you, I guess. What are you still doing here? I thought you said you had work to do."

"I have a mountain of work to do, but you said donuts, and who can turn down donuts?" He grabbed another one off the table. "Plus, I figured I owed you one for messing up your morning."

"Thank you." Natalie asked before she sipped her refilled mug.

"You're welcome."

Natalie smiled, shaking her head. "Time to go get the kids," she said, making an exit.

Chapter Twelve

Ben finished putting the last of their clothes up in their suitcase before him and Hannah headed to the hotel lobby to eat breakfast. The weekend had gone by way too fast and they were hoping to savor every last minute they had with just the two of them. Hannah pressed the elevator button for the lobby. Ben wrapped his arms around her and she leaned back into his chest. She tilted her head to the side and he leaned in and kissed her. She made a mental note to not get too distracted with the kids and work when she got home to miss out on these moments. Their marriage needed this. It needed them to keep making an effort. To keep dating and keep flirting. They enjoyed their meal of egg benedicts and mimosa, before heading back to their room to get their suitcase and check out.

"I got a text from my mom this morning. What's our plan for Christmas? Are we going to their house or do you want them to come to ours?" Ben asked as Hannah was putting on her makeup. She paused as she set down the mascara.

"I don't know yet," Hannah said, already feeling defeated. Her least favorite part of the holiday was making plans. No matter how hard she tried, someone got left out, someone's feelings got hurt, and to top it off she was pretty sure she'd be stuck at work on Christmas Day.

"Okay, okay, that's fine. I didn't mean to stress you out," he said as he walked over to her. "No need to figure it all out now, we are still on vacation."

"Christmas is only three weeks away," she said with a sigh.

"Plenty of time to decide," he reassured her.

"If you say so." Hannah's mind immediately went to her endless to-do list. Three weeks to finish all the shopping, the cleaning, the kids' school projects, their Christmas programs. What was she forgetting? She racked her brain as she finished putting on her mascara.

They walked to the car in the parking lot. Ben lifted the suitcase into the trunk and they headed back on their two-hour drive. As they were on the road, traffic bottlenecked. Ben started asking about their Christmas plans again.

"I mean we did spend Thanksgiving with your family, so it'd be nice if we could spend Christmas with mine," he added.

"I thought you didn't want to do this now." Hannah's tone was short. She was ready to get home and see the kids, and making plans for Christmas was the last thing on her mind.

Ben pushed back. "What's so wrong with my parents coming to our house for Christmas?"

"What's wrong with that? What if I'm at the hospital working while everyone is at home unwrapping gifts? The kids won't want to wait on me to get home. Not to mention the time I'll have to spend getting the house ready while you're away traveling for most of the month. That's not fair to ask of me."

"What's not fair is that you always decide for us what we're going to do for the holidays. I'll help clean for their visit like I always do. " Ben said. "If the roles were reversed I'd do the same."

"Well isn't that convenient." Hannah threw her hands up. "You don't have to be in my shoes, because I don't have parents anymore."

Then Hannah burst into tears. After a few minutes of silence while also going twenty miles an hour on the interstate Ben pulled the car over and broke the tension with a whisper.

"That's what you're really upset about isn't it? Your parents? Amy?" he asked.

Hannah nodded.

Her voice croaked out a whisper. "I thought it was going to get easier. I thought it wouldn't hurt as much that they're not here but every Christmas. Every holiday. It still just hurts."

With his left hand on the steering wheel, he reached his right hand over to Hannah's lap and squeezed her hands she had clutched together. She looked up at him and offered a weak smile.

"Look, maybe we can do our family Christmas a few days early when I don't have to work and then you can invite your parents to visit and I won't feel so left out," Hannah conceded.

"We can figure it out and work together. I know Christmas hasn't been easy for you, but I want our kids to have a great Christmas. That's what your parents would want," he said.

Hannah took a deep breath and nodded. That was absolutely what her parents would want.

* * *

On one hand, Natalie was relieved to see Ben and Hannah pull into the driveway. She was exhausted from the weekend. She had no idea that taking care of kids was so tiring, especially overnight. On the other hand, she was a little disappointed her time with Eli was about to come to an end. He drove her nuts, but he made her laugh like she hadn't laughed in years. She couldn't stay mad at him. He was too cute for that.

"How was your trip?" Natalie asked as Hannah and Ben entered through the garage pulling their suitcase.

"It was good," Hannah answered before she yelled out for the kids.

"Oh, Eli took them on a walk. They had energy to burn. I made sure they wore their coats and gloves. They should be back any minute."

Ben left the kitchen in a hurry. Natalie raised her eyebrow.

"Don't ask," Hannah said as she turned.

"What time do you need me next week?" Natalie asked.

"I'm being so rude. I'm sorry. We had a great trip for the most part until the ride home. Lots of traffic," she answered. "How were the kids? Did they behave?" she asked.

"They did. They really are great kids," Natalie answered. "Besides Eli came over and helped out some."

Hannah looked surprised. "Really?"

Natalie nodded, trying to hide her smile.

* * *

Natalie left shortly before Eli returned with the kids.

Quinn and Luke immediately embraced their mom at the same time as though she had been gone for more than two nights.

Eli grabbed his car keys off the counter.

"Natalie already left?"

"Yeah, she just left. She needed to get a meeting. So you and Natalie were holding down the fort while we were gone?"

Eli nodded. "She was overwhelmed with the kids' soccer schedule and I wasn't busy."

Hannah shook her head and laughed. "Look, I know it's been a while since what's her name? Please don't do anything to mess things up with Natalie. The kids really like her and I do too, okay?"

"You don't have to worry about anything like that. We're only friends. I guess. I'm not interested in dating her," he said, not even believing himself.

Quinn walked back in the kitchen to grab an apple out of the fruit bowl on the counter. "Yeah, Natalie would never date Uncle Eli. He messed up her pretty red blouse before she was supposed to sing the solo at church."

"What?" Hannah turned toward Eli.

"It was a little harmless prank. Thanks for ratting me out kid," he play-

73

fully shook his head at her.

Quinn took a bite of the apple, "You're welcome," she said, her mouth full.

"Don't go teaching my kids things from when you were little."

"I won't, I promise. At least not anymore," he cracked a smile.

"Eli."

He shrugged. Hannah gave him a hug.

"Well I'm still happy to have you in town. Bad influence and all." She smiled.

"Me too." Eli grinned.

Chapter Thirteen

Natalie was thankful for a reason to get up from her desk and take a movement break at work. Her morning had consisted of hundreds of data entries for their festival of tree biddings. She walked down the street from the hospital to meet Mrs. Nelson at their favorite coffee shop. The sun was shining but the air felt brisk for the middle of December. She passed many shoppers taking advantage of the beautiful day to eat and shop downtown.

Since moving to Harbor Ridge, Mrs. Sandy Nelson had been a mentor for Natalie. When Natalie got her first job and moved off campus, Mrs. Nelson rented a townhouse to Natalie. Every once and a while Mrs. Nelson would stop by and drop off freshly baked bread and goodies, and whenever it was Natalie's birthday, she would bring flowers over. Mrs. Nelson had a son who went to school states away, and while she missed her son, she loved filling her days volunteering and doing small gestures of kindness to other people. Becoming an empty nester became a catalyst for Sandy to try something new. She'd decided to take on the responsibility of organizing the whole Live Nativity when her son had left for college.

Natalie immediately spotted Mrs. Nelson sitting in a corner booth of the cafe. Her dark hair with gray streaks barely peeked over the booth. Mrs. Nelson's smile was contagious and could be seen a mile away. She was a petite woman but her voice carried the volume of someone twice her size. Mrs. Nelson stood up from the booth when she noticed Natalie. The two embraced before sitting back down across from one another.

"We are almost fully cast for the Live Nativity and have all the contracts filed for the rest of the festival. In the ten years I've been putting on the event, this was the first year we've had enough people this early on to fill the many roles for their Nativity," Mrs. Nelson said gleefully as she stirred her coffee. She continued, "Several families who have children in the musical have also signed up. You're doing such a good job with rehearsals."

"Thank you. I'm excited. That's fantastic about the casting, and we're less than three weeks away," Natalie said. "I'm so excited for the musical next week. I think the kids are doing a great job."

"It's been fun having you with the team this year. I called city hall yesterday to check on our permit and the secretary told me that there's been a delay since the flu outbreak, but that our permit and funding request should be handled by the end of next week."

Maybe I should ask Eli about it, Natalie thought. It would be nice to get this taken care of.

"Perfect. Are you getting ready for the holidays? When is Matt coming in from school?"

A huge smile emerged on Sandy's face. "I usually put my decorations up in November. I've enjoyed having the decorations up. Truthfully, if he'd let me I'd keep them up all year long." She laughed so hard the people sitting around them turned around to look.

"I know what you mean. It's so much work to put up all of the decorations to only enjoy them for a short time." Natalie thought of growing up and how her parents made tree decorating such a fun experience. They would have a big breakfast and then get to work unpacking all the ornaments passed down to them or bought on special vacations. Their tree was their own personal scrapbook.

"Matt will finish exams this week. He is bringing his girlfriend with him to meet me," Mrs. Nelson said.

"At Christmas? Things must be serious between them, then."

"Right?" Sandy raised her hands to her face. Her voice got louder.

76

"That's what I said. I told him to think long and hard about it because this sends a strong signal to her."

"What did he say to that?" Natalie had met Matt a few times over the years and each time he seemed to be even-keeled.

Sandy stirred her drink with her straw and looked up, "He said he knew and that he wanted me to meet her. She's very special to him."

"Good for him."

Natalie hoped the smile on her face hid her disappointment. She too had once been introduced to someone's family as "someone special" and even had a ring on her finger to prove it. That had been a long time ago, and she pushed away the painful memories.

"I feel a little nervous, truth be told. He's never brought a girl home before from college," Sandy said.

"Has Matt met her parents?"

"No, sadly both of her parents passed away when she was in high school. He did say that he met her aunt and uncle and a few cousins at Thanksgiving," Sandy answered.

"I'm sure they loved him. He's a nice guy."

"Thank you. I always said I don't care whether my kid makes a ton of money or drives fancy cars, I just want to raise a decent human being." Sandy smiled.

"And you have succeeded. Matt's a good guy." Natalie smiled back.

"I can't take too much credit. I did my best. I've been praying for his wife since he was a little boy. You know Matt's dad left when he was five and it's just been the two of us for quite some time. I hope he's not being seduced into anything he's not ready for." Sandy shook her head.

"You think it's that serious?"

"Can you keep a secret? Don't tell Matt I told you," Sandy whispered as she looked around the coffee shop.

"Of course," Natalie said.

"He asked me if he could have my mother's engagement ring."

"That sounds serious. Are you going to give it to him?"

Sandy sighed. "I'm not sure. My mother did leave it for him. He's the only grandchild. I'm honestly surprised he wants it, but it is a gorgeous ring. Guess we'll find out when they get to Harbor Ridge this weekend." Sandy looked at her watch. "I've got to leave in fifteen minutes and I've wasted most of the time not talking about what we came here to talk about. I'm sorry. Sometimes I can get a little carried away."

Natalie quietly laughed to herself. *That is an understatement.*

"I understand. You have a lot going on with the Festival and Matt coming into town. I am happy to help all I can. I'm excited to be a part of the event again this year. It's one of my favorite parts of Christmas."

Sandy reached her hand across the table and grabbed Natalie's. "You have been such a help to me these past few years. If you can stay on top of our friends at city hall, that would be a huge help. They changed our contact there since the city manager resigned." Sandy opened a beige filing folder and flipped through a few pages. "Here it is. Our contact is Eli Collins. You've met him?"

Natalie felt her face flush.

"Yes I've . . . we've met a few times." She tilted her face down to keep her smile from being seen.

"Great, then we're on our way."

On her walk back to work, Natalie thought about when she might get to see Eli again. *Now I just get to keep hounding the guy who doesn't like Christmas.*

Meeting up with Sandy had taken longer than she anticipated and Natalie had to grab a salad on her way back so she could eat at her desk.

Natalie loved the holidays: the music playing over every loudspeaker, the festive decorations, the delicious food. Even with those feelings, sometimes Natalie still wanted to speed up the holidays. Mostly work. Juggling the hospital job with working out and occasionally babysitting, plus helping with the Festival of Trees, was starting to take its toll. *This too shall pass.* The weeks and months of her work would culminate to the beautiful night of the Festival and it would all be worth it. Then would come the week off for Christmas and she'd be able to visit with her family.

As Natalie took a bite of her salad, Rachel walked over to her desk. "How was your weekend? Was this the weekend you had the kids?"

"It was."

Natalie smiled, thinking about the fun she shared with the kids and especially Eli. He drove her crazy and just when she was about to lose it, he would say something sweet and make everything better. "How was your weekend?"

Rachel dropped her shoulders and sighed. "Another date with someone who was, shall we say, quite ambitious in both their profile picture and bio. The meal was good, but the company was a waste."

"You'll find the right guy. He's out there somewhere."

"You'll find the right guy too. If you haven't already." Rachel winked at her.

Natalie couldn't keep a straight face. "What? No. I'm … well." Her smile gave her away. Making excuses was not going to work with Rachel, who was desperate to set her up and always noticed everything.

Rachel's eyes widened with enthusiasm. "Who is it?"

Natalie's shoulders shrugged. "No one. Not really."

It can't be anything. Who knew how long Eli would even be in Harbor Ridge? Did he feel the same way? He even made some remark that she reminded him of his sister. Not exactly what she wanted to hear. Guess they were just destined to be friends.

"If you say so," Rachel said. "But this morning you walked in with the biggest smile on your face, and you'll have to tell me who put it there someday."

Natalie couldn't help herself and finally spilled the beans.

"You remember I was babysitting for Quinn and Luke over the weekend, right? Well their uncle lives in town, Hannah's twin brother, and he came by to visit some and help out with the kids."

Rachel's eyes got even bigger. "And he's the reason for the smile?"

"I don't know. Maybe. I guess. He's frustrating but generous and funny. At times."

"Anything wrong with him?"

"He seems quite sure of himself."

"And that's a bad thing?"

"No, but it doesn't even matter," Natalie said unsure of where it would even go given the chance.

Chapter Fourteen

Eli slowly pulled into the church's parking lot. The glare of the moon reflected the church's white steeple. This time of year had always been Eli's least favorite. It was dark when he went into work and dark when he got out of the office. He was hoping for a little brightness tonight.

That always seemed to happen when he saw Natalie. She had a way of making everything better and brighter. He found her demeanor annoying at first, but he soon realized it was because she was far different than him. And that wasn't a bad thing. She was tender-hearted but guarded. He wondered what had made her that way. Maybe one day they would get close enough and he could ask her.

The streetlights illuminated the parking lot and Eli had to circle twice before finally squeezing into a space. His sister's van was wider and longer than his Tesla. Plus he was driving with two extra pieces of precious cargo. Eli held onto Luke's and Quinn's hand as he walked with them through the busy parking lot at church. Luke looked side to side.

"Where is Mommy? I thought she was coming."

Eli stopped and turned around before crouching down to Luke's level. He had learned to do that by watching Natalie with the children. She was so good with them. He was looking forward to seeing her again tonight.

"Your mommy is at the hospital finishing her shift. She will be here as soon as she can. You need to make sure you smile really big so she can see it when she gets here."

"Like this?" Luke grinned as wide as his seven-year-old mouth would let him.

Eli smiled back. "Exactly like that." Quinn saw one of her friends in the parking lot and joined her and her family.

Luke turned to catch up with Quinn and her friends. Hannah was going to meet them there after her shift. Ben was traveling for work and couldn't make it. Natalie had offered to take the kids with her but that would have meant the kids would be there hours before the performance. Eli had told Hannah he wasn't busy, because he didn't want the kids to have to wait around for hours. Besides, he wanted to spend as much time with Quinn and Luke while he could. Who knew where his next assignment would take him, and then how often he could see them then?

Organized mass chaos was how Eli would describe the scene in the gym. The church called it something different, though.

The Children's Christmas Pageant.

This is where the children were supposed to meet while they got into the groups for their role. There were at least fifty children dressed in various characters with twelve adult volunteers. Eli stood in line to check in the kids. He quickly gazed the room again to see if Natalie was around, and felt a twinge of disappointment that she was not. After signing Luke and Quinn's name to the paper, he headed out a different door to find the sanctuary.

Eli made the quick walk under the awning to the sanctuary where the performance would take place. After walking around the church for a few minutes, he peeked his head in a door with the light on.

"Excuse me? Can you point me to the sanctuary?"

Natalie stood up. "Eli? You scared me!" Natalie put her hands down on the chair in front of her to stabilize herself. "I thought I was alone."

"Sorry I saw the light was on. I am totally lost."

"You and me both."

Eli raised his eyebrow. "I thought you went to this church?"

Natalie smiled and scrunched her nose. He loved when she did that. "I do, I just mean I feel lost about what I'm about to do. Directing this Christmas pageant. I've never felt so nervous about anything in my life."

Eli walked over and put his hands on her shoulders. "Fifty crazy kids. What could go wrong?" He smirked.

Natalie backed up from him and let his hands fall back to his sides. "Hey now. I thought you'd be helping me?"

"It won't be perfect, but what in life ever is? It will still be good. Luke and Quinn have been talking about this for weeks. You will do great."

Natalie's eyes looked up from the floor and met his gaze. *How have we not kissed before?* Natalie looked down at her phone.

She quickly stood up and almost lost her balance. "Oh, I've got to go and get the kids ready to line up."

"Natalie. The sanctuary?"

"Oh right." She pointed her finger down the long hallway. "Go all the way to the end of this hallway and go up two flights of stairs. It's on your left."

"Thank you."

Eli made his way to the sanctuary and found a seat toward the back. Some excited parents and grandparents monopolized the first few pews but Eli was more than happy to sit in the balcony. Hannah, dressed in her lavender scrubs and her hair pulled back in a ponytail. came in ten minutes later, right before the play began. Her face told the story of having a long day at the hospital. Eli waved as Hannah's eyes searched the sanctuary.

Soon the lights dimmed and there was movement on stage in the darkness. A bright fluorescent light illuminated Natalie as she stood off to the side of the stage. Natalie walked up to the microphone as the audience continued applauding. Eli couldn't keep his eyes off her as the silver embellishments sparkled under the lights.

"Good evening, I'm Natalie Walker. Welcome to this year's Christmas play. It has been a joy to work with your children. Please join us for a reception after the concert for some refreshments in the gymnasium. If you enjoy yourself this evening, please make plans to join us at the Festival of Trees celebration December 22nd. We will have a table set up at the reception after tonight's performance for more information. Thank you!"

Natalie sat in the front pew along with three other volunteers, directing the motions the whole time. Eli noticed the way she overacted the facial expressions so the children could see her in the back. Her smile widened with each song finishing. She clearly loved every moment she spent with the children. When one child misbehaved, all it took was one loud snap and point and the child stopped in his tracks.

"What are you smiling about?" Hannah asked him in between songs.

Eli blushed. "Nothing."

At the conclusion of the concert, the children were escorted off the stage to head back to the gym where Eli had dropped them off. Hannah and Eli slowly made their way behind the throngs of parents and grandparents.

"Thanks again for bringing Quinn and Luke tonight." Hannah said before a big yawn. "Sorry, it's getting close to my bedtime." Eli laughed.

"Of course. Not a problem at all. The kids were adorable tonight."

"They sure were. I can't wait to send some of the videos to Ben when we get home."

The gymnasium was decked out in everything Christmas. There was a cookie decorating station, making a Rudolph with popsicle sticks, googly eyes and red pom poms, and an ornament making station.

Natalie and Sandy stood by a table handing out flyers advertising their Live Nativity in a few weeks and asking for volunteers.

Eli did his best to slide by unannounced to avoid getting volunteered, but Quinn went right up to Natalie.

"I want to be a sheep. My mom said I was a great sheep," Quinn announced so most of the gym could hear.

Natalie smiled and knelt down to Quinn's level, eye-to-eye.

"You would be a great sheep. Did you know we'll have real sheep there, too?"

Quinn's eyes got really big before she looked confused. "I can still be one too though, right?" she asked.

"Of course," Natalie looked up at Eli and smiled. "But what will Uncle Eli be?"

Eli put his hands up and shook his head.

Quinn got a big smile on her face.

"He can be a shepherd! Right Uncle Eli?"

Eli mouthed *thanks a lot* to Natalie. She winked back at him.

"You're welcome," Natalie responded with a smile as she handed him a flyer, which Eli took reluctantly.

Great, Eli thought.

Work had been exhausting and so had been helping Hannah and Ben with the kids. The last thing he needed was another obligation during this time of year. He would at least get to see Natalie again, so that was a bonus. He found himself wanting to be where she was.

"Mommy, Mommy," Quinn exclaimed. "Uncle Eli and I are going to be in the Live Nativity! Won't you come, please?"

Hannah looked down at the flyer.

"We'll see, but now it's time to head home and go to bed." She grabbed Quinn's hand and looked around for Eli and Luke.

As they walked out to their car, Eli noticed Natalie walking out to the parking lot at the same time. Hannah and the kids walked ahead. He held the door open for her.

"You're heading out?" he asked.

"Yep, it's been a long day. Sandy will stay and finish up with the rest of the kids and parents. I've been here since three this afternoon," she answered, trying unsuccessfully to stifle a yawn.

"I was going to grab some dinner at Luigi's if you want to come?" Eli said so quickly Natalie wasn't sure she heard him correctly.

"Oh, um, sure, that would be fun," she answered with a smile. "I haven't eaten anything since breakfast this morning. I was too busy and nervous."

"I don't know why you were so nervous. You did great tonight."

Their eyes met as Eli gave her hand a squeeze. They walked in silence to his car. Hannah had driven his car to work so they could switch when the pageant was over.

* * *

Natalie wasn't sure why she felt nervous. She and Eli had been together before many times over the past few weeks. Those times had been arranged by her schedule with the kids, though. This time he had made a point to ask her out. Alone.

She hadn't been on a date in years. Why did she have to say yes? Was it even a date? Maybe he just wanted to get something to eat. Natalie's stomach began to knot up as she overthought like usual.

Eli opened the passenger door for her. She looked up at him and smiled.

"Unless of course, you'd rather sit in the back like before," he joked.

She smiled softly as she slid in the seat. "No, this is perfect."

Eli smiled back at her as he gently closed the car door and they made the five minute ride to the diner.

The bells chimed on the door of the diner as Eli opened it for Natalie. He blew in his hands to warm them up. "It's freezing."

"It sure is." Natalie nodded.

They walked to the hostess stand. A young woman with strawberry blonde hair tied in a high ponytail and a fitted apron over her jeans and sweatshirt held out two menus.

"Right this way," a waitress said, pointing to the table in the back corner.

"After you." Eli motioned for Natalie to walk ahead of him. He put his hand at the top of her back as they walked to their table.

After the waitress brought their coffee, Eli wasted no time taking a sip. Natalie hummed along to the festive song playing over the sound system and gazed out the window at the snow flurries. Her eyes lit up as she touched the snow globe at the end of the table. She tipped it upside down before setting it back on the table.

"So you seem to really like Christmas?"

Natalie stirred her coffee and took a sip. "You seem to hate it?" She peeled back the foil on the top of the creamer before slowly pouring it in the mug.

"I don't hate it . . ." Eli said slowly.

Natalie grinned. "That's a relief. How can anyone hate Christmas?" She gently blew on her coffee before taking a sip.

Eli tilted his head. "I just don't get the appeal."

"Right, all the yummy food, giving to others, the carols, the decorations. Who would like all of that?" she answered sarcastically.

"Come on, if only it worked that way. It's like the universe walks around in some festive fog from Thanksgiving to New Years', cutting people off in traffic," he nodded toward her, " or in parking lots . . ."

She felt her face blush. He had touched a nerve. "You're really going to go there?" Natalie sneered as she set her coffee down ready to go toe to toe with him.

"Stores use Christmas to sell love and happiness like we should all be linking arms and singing kumbaya," Eli finished.

"Did you ever think you find what you're looking for? If you're looking for the stress and angst of the Christmas season, you'll find that."

"Don't have to look far."

She picked up the snowglobe and slid it over to him. "But, if you look for the wonder, the magic, the hope and the beauty of it. You can find that too."

"Maybe. I've gotten so tired of having to find the perfect Christmas gift and if it's not exactly what they want or it costs an arm and a leg they get upset about it. It's those stupid jewelry commercials, the mistletoe, those cheesy holiday movies." He gave her a side eye as he said it. " That's why I stopped dating from Halloween to Valentine's Day. I hate all of it. The expectations and drama."

That explains so much, Natalie thought.

She wanted to tell him she sometimes felt the same way. She had been heartbroken during the holidays before and knew how he must be feeling. It didn't have to be that way. He could make new memories, but what good would that do. He seemed to be set in his ways. He hated Christmas.

"Quinn seemed to enjoy the Christmas pageant. She can't stop talking about it and the Festival of Trees," Natalie said.

Eli shrugged. "She's young. Hasn't had time to be jaded."

"Maybe her enthusiasm will rub off on you," she joked.

"Nah, I'm just looking forward to a few days off from work and then I'm heading to Colorado to go skiing with some buddies of mine. What are you doing for Christmas?" he asked.

Natalie smiled. "I'm meeting up with my brother's family. My parents are coming, too. I'm flying out on Christmas Day since the festival is on the 22nd."

"Why does it feel like December tries to cram in as much stuff as possible?"

Natalie nodded in agreement. "I know what you mean. I feel like I can barely keep up with everything I have going on.

"How's your job going?"

"It's going all right. Like you said, this time of year is so busy. Sometimes it feels like I barely have any down time. The hospital is handling the tree part for the festival and then I'm working with Sandy on the Live Nativity. There are a few moving parts, and making sure all of them are getting done can be a challenge."

"If you weren't at the hospital, what would you want to do?"

"Maybe something in education. That was my major before I transferred colleges."

"You transferred? How come?"

Natalie looked down at her coffee mug. She wondered if this was the right time to go into when her personal life got off track. She had still not gotten it back to where she wanted it to be, and wasn't sure if it could happen for her again.

As quickly as he asked the question she answered softly. "I was engaged and the wedding didn't happen. I needed to move on."

Eli's eyes widened before he quickly changed the subject. "You like your job at the hospital?" Natalie was glad to move on from the subject as well. It was awkward.

"There's a job opening at the hospital but it's fulltime and it would mean cutting back on watching Quinn and Luke. And all of the volunteer stuff I like to do."

"Are you happy with how things are?"

Natalie looked around the room. *Happy enough.* She wasn't sure what she really wanted. She thought she did a long time ago and the rug was pulled out from under her. She was determined to never be blindsided like that again.

"I like where things are now."

She looked across the table at him and smiled.

"You should go for the job. If that's what you want."

Natalie tucked a stray hair behind her ear. "What if I apply and don't get it? It would be awkward to go back to work knowing that I wanted the job I didn't get." She took another sip of coffee, "Does moving around so much for your job ever bother you?"

His eyes searched for clarity, "Does what bother me?"

"Not being able to make friends or have a support system in the same place if you're not in town very long?"

"I like moving from place to place. It keeps things exciting. And I have friends."

Natalie sighed. "I'm sorry—that came out wrong. I just meant, it must be difficult to move around frequently and still have a relationship."

His tone turned serious. "It can be difficult, but I believe staying in the same place could be just as difficult."

He took a long sip of coffee.

"Now one thing I don't like about moving around so much is the constant unpacking."

Natalie smiled at him and he smiled back. "How is the unpacking going?

Made any more progress?"

Eli began to nod his head before laughing and shaking it. "Not really. Getting settled is not my strong suite."

"Do you need me to come over and help again?"

He smiled. "I'd like that."

"Me too."

Their conversation continued to flow until they were the last diners left.

"I had fun tonight. Thanks for dinner."

"No problem. Thanks for joining me."

He helped her put her black coat on. They walked to his car. Eli went back into the diner to retrieve one of his gloves. As Natalie looked down at the floorboard, she noticed the glove.

He came back declaring he had found it. Must have been a different pair, Natalie thought.

They continued their conversation during the brief drive back to their complex.

"Thanks for dinner. I'll have to return the favor sometime."

"I'd like that."

Natalie smiled as she walked up the sidewalk to her front door. As she turned her keys in her front door, she turned and waved bye to Eli. He smiled at her.

Chapter Fifteen

Sandy sat nervously at the arrivals gate as passengers from the West Coast arrived. She looked up as a throng of passengers came down the escalator and stairs at the time her son's flight was due to arrive. She'd had this date marked on her calendar for months—from the moment Matt had gone away to college, in fact. This was his final year away and she was eager to have him move back home after graduation. There were several companies in town that were interested in him. Sandy had already been asking around.

She stood from her chair with an eager anticipation. Even though her son had been away at college for three and a half years, each goodbye was still as tough as the first time he left.

Each hello was that much sweeter.

Her eyes noticed the Lakers hat in the distance. Her boy was home.

Her son, Matt, walked hand in hand with a beautiful, petite young woman. He towered over her frame and the top of her head barely reached his shoulder. As they reached the bottom of the escalator, he broke from her hand and embraced his mom. Sandy did her best to keep her tears at bay.

"Welcome home!" she said as a few tears dripped down.

He pulled back and put his arm around his girlfriend.

"Mom, I want you to meet my girlfriend Amy," he said with a smile.

Sandy hugged her.

"It's nice to finally meet you. I've heard a lot about you," Sandy smiled warmly. She had noticed Amy in the background of the video calls she had with Matt once a week or so, but Amy had usually been shy about joining the call.

Amy smiled back and softly replied, "It's nice to meet you too."

"I bet you both are starving. Would you like to get barbecue for dinner?" It's Matt's favorite . . ."

"Actually, Mom I've been meaning to tell you. I'm a vegan now."

"A what?"

"A vegan."

"Like you don't eat meat anymore, or something crazy like that?"

Amy chimed in. "Actually, many people in *our* generation realize the effect eating meat has on global warming and no longer indulge in the consumption of any animal products."

And with that Sandy's dream Christmas meal was in the garbage. All of the weeks she spent digging through her recipe books and looking online to create the perfect meal. All of the recipes used butter and cheese. They *always* had ham. Amy was a vegan and had clearly brainwashed her son into the same thing.

As the three of them were waiting for their suitcase to arrive, Amy excused herself to go to the bathroom. Sandy sat down on one of the benches.

"I wish you would have told me that you stopped eating meat," she said.

"And dairy, eggs and . . ." Matt added.

"Yes, all of that," Sandy put her head in her hands. "What am I supposed to do with all of the food I'm making for our Christmas dinner? What about all of your favorite snacks I bought that you *used* to eat." She looked around before adding, "You know Matt, you shouldn't have to change yourself to get some girl to like you."

"Mom, she's not some girl. She's my girlfriend, I'm hoping to ask her to marry me," he said.

"Well that's just crazy. You haven't known her very long at all."

"Because you and Dad dated for how long again?"

Sandy took a deep breath. "Matthew Stephen Nelson."

"Mom, I'm a grownup."

"Whose mother still pays for your tuition, gas and car insurance. Not a grown up," she added.

"Mom, I want to have a good Christmas. Please," he pleaded.

"I want that too. I just don't know what I'm going to do with all of that food," she sighed.

"Oh I'm sure Amy can help you with some new recipes," he assured her.

Sandy huffed in disappointment as she stood up from the uncomfortable metal chair. Just then Amy arrived back as their suitcase passed them on the conveyor belt. Matt went to go fetch it. Amy and Sandy stood in the awkward silence, either one knowing what to say.

"Let's go," Matt announced once he had the suitcase.

"Great, let's go," both ladies answered simultaneously. Both relieved to be moving on from their awkward start.

Chapter Sixteen

With a few weeks before Christmas and rumors continuing about Linda's retirement on the horizon, Linda's attendance at meetings for the festival were becoming more and more sparse. Rachel and Natalie began trading off duties for who would take notes for each meeting while the other would chime in on reporting to their director about the status of the festival.

"Any fun plans this weekend?" Rachel asked with anticipation.

Natalie slid her laptop and her thick three-ring binder into her shoulder bag. She had to shimmy the binder to get her bag to zip.

"You mean besides all the work we have to do?" Natalie blew a stray hair out of her face.

Rachel covered her eyes with her hands. "I can't look at those spreadsheets again."

"I know what you mean. This has always been my least favorite part of the festival, but we are almost to the finish line."

"Still you should have some fun planned this weekend."

Natalie shrugged her shoulders. "I'm going to Luke's soccer game tomorrow. He's playing in the championship game. A bunch of seven-year-olds running after a soccer ball. It's super cute."

"Will Luke's super cute uncle be there too?"

Natalie looked down to the monitor as she turned it off and could feel her face become warm. She looked up to Rachel who smiled.

"I'll take that as a yes."

Natalie shook her head before breaking out in a smile. Rachel liked to tease her.

"Have a good weekend," Natalie said as she flung her bag over her shoulder.

"You too. Have fun on your *not* a date."

* * *

Eli woke up early on Saturday to make it into the Chamber of Commerce for his eight a.m. meeting. He had come back with recommendations for the city to implement in the New Year and the board was eager to turn things around and wanted to hear from Eli right away.

Eli sat opposite the three members of Harbor Ridge's city council in the windowless conference room. The chill from outside was evident in the cold reception Eli received when he walked into the room.

A computer screen behind him showed the slides regarding his recommendations.

Eli took a quick sip of his warm coffee before diving into his report.

"The city's budget is in crisis. If we want to start the New Year in a good place for Harbor Ridge, we need to implement some cuts, and now."

The mayor took off his glasses and put them down on his open folder. "You're suggesting we get rid of the Christmas celebrations in Harbor Ridge?"

Eli referred back to his Powerpoint. "No, that's not what I'm saying or suggesting. Some events are more profitable than others. The Christmas Tree Lighting on the twentieth, for example, charges twelve dollars for admission. The city makes money on that event. Others, such as the Live Nativity and the Harbor Ridge Hospital Festival of Trees, do not charge admission but also utilize thousands of dollars in police for street closings, etc. I would charge admission."

He noticed the mayor and staff taking notes.

Eli wondered if he should tip Natalie off. Ultimately, it was a work decision, nothing personal. Besides, maybe she'd be relieved to have a night off. He felt like a coward. What good would it do to say anything before it was final? There was chance they'd keep the festival in the budget if they charged an admission fee. It wasn't his call to make.

Eli ended the meeting a little after ten o'clock. The mayor and his staff would discuss his recommendations and then make a decision later in the week. He quickly got in his car and headed to the indoor soccer complex. He hoped he hadn't missed Luke scoring a goal.

He arrived and noticed Ben and Hannah sitting with Quinn. Quinn was occupied coloring princess pages on the bleachers with her back turned to him. The field was chaotic and the other team's coach called a timeout. Eli sat down next to Hannah.

"Natalie didn't come?"

Hannah looked at him. "Nice to see you too."

Eli playfully elbowed her. "Sorry, I'm glad to see you."

Eli smiled to himself. He noticed Natalie walking down the bleachers toward them with a coffee in her hand. "I should have asked if you wanted something. I didn't know if you were coming, " Natalie said apologetically.

"I already ate. I had a breakfast meeting but I wanted to come cheer on Luke. Thanks though."

Hannah, stuck in the middle with the two of them talking over her, decided to stand up and sit next to Ben.

Ben asked Hannah, "We're still on for my company Christmas party?"

"When it is again?" Hannah racked her brain trying to remember.

"It's in two weeks."

"Natalie, are you available to babysit? I hadn't planned on going to his work's Christmas party but Ben's work trip got canceled for that weekend."

Natalie shook her head. "I'm sorry I can't that night. I have the Chamber dinner. I also signed up to go with my admin team for the hospital or I would."

"You're going to the Chamber dinner?" Eli chimed in.

"I was planning to. Are you?"

"I'm supposed to, I guess. One of the aldermen can't make it because his son has a band concert that night, so he gave me his ticket. Well, he gave me two tickets."

Natalie looked at Eli inquisitively. "You do know that there will be lots of Christmas music and Santa might be making an appearance? I didn't think it would be your thing."

Eli put his hands into his jean pockets before hanging his head and softly saying, "Would you want to go with me?"

"Huh?" Natalie asked.

Eli looked up at her, his hands still in his pockets. He felt like he was sixteen again about to ask his crush to the high school dance. He cleared his throat. "Would you like to be my guest at the Chamber dinner next weekend?"

"As a date?" Hannah chimed in.

Why did she have to say that? Eli stared her down before turning his attention back to Natalie, whose face was matching the color of her red sweater. His eyes softened. "I don't know anyone else going. You could save me from all the awkward small talk? Please?"

Natalie tucked a stray hair behind her ear. "Oh okay. Way to twist my arm." Natalie opened the calendar app on her phone.

"Actually Hannah, I had the dates wrong. The Chamber dinner is the week before your party so I can babysit for you."

Hannah couldn't contain her excitement and clapped her hands together. "That would be perfect. I've always wanted to go to one of Ben's company's parties but haven't yet. Thank you!"

The crowd erupted into cheers. Luke's team won. The teams lined up to shake each others' hands.

Eli turned to Natalie, Hannah and the group.

"Let's go celebrate."

"I can't, I'm sorry. I have way too much work to do for the festival. Tell Luke how proud of him I am."

"We will. I know he's so glad you got to come watch." Ben answered.

Natalie's eyes met Eli's as she walked down the bleachers. She could feel his eyes stay on her as she left the gym. She wanted to go to lunch and keep talking with Eli, but she knew the more work she could get done on Saturday, the easier her work week would be.

Chapter Seventeen

Natalie parked in the farthest lot at the shopping mall. She had a break from work and decided to get some shopping done. She adopted two angels from the angel tree from the hospital lobby, a boy and a girl. These children were in foster care and in some cases the gifts they received through this program might be the only gifts they receive at all. As a kid, it had been a family tradition to go shopping for an angel tree child. Natalie's parents had always tried to instill in her and her brother the true meaning of Christmas and sharing their love with those less fortunate. Giving always blessed the giver as much if not more than the receiver.

As much as Natalie tried to let go of the hurt she felt over her broken heart, Christmas was always a reminder of what she didn't have. It had been four years since her almost-wedding, and seeing all of the couples walking hand in hand in the mall and the moms pushing strollers while juggling their big bags of presents still stung a little all these years later. In time, Natalie came to understand that her ex-fiance calling off their wedding had been a blessing in disguise. He wasn't who she thought he was and while it had been humiliating for him to have called off the wedding the day after the invitations went out, she was thankful they never got married.

On what would have been her first wedding anniversary, Natalie saw a news story about a bride who donated all the food from her canceled reception to a homeless shelter. The bride granted an interview to a local news station and said she decided to donate the food because otherwise it would go to waste and that she wanted something good to come from her heart being broken. She wanted to continue the tradition her parents had instilled in her. To always look for the silver lining. For the reminder that God could use our hurt for something greater.

In time, Natalie felt the same way about her canceled wedding and was desperate to take back the terrible memories she had of the day he ended it. It was as though there was an invisible line drawn in her life. Who she was before that day would never be the same. To have to fend off rumors and the looks from people when she went out. Leaving college was the best thing she ever did to move on. Sure, it hadn't been easy starting over and slowly building connections and friendships, but after three years at Harbor Ridge, she was proud of the life she had. It felt safe and mundane. She liked knowing what to expect and what was coming.

She stood in line at the crowded coffee cart for a steaming cup of hot chocolate to warm herself up before she headed to the department store to chip away at her list.

Natalie passed two jewelry stores that were advertising special discounts on engagement rings, necklaces, and earrings. She was the last single person in her friend group from college. Her own mother seemed to have given up on sending anymore hints or asking for updates on Natalie's social life.

She tried to not look but avoiding any sign of love, weddings and romance was too difficult these days. Christmas and love went together.

And for Natalie, so did heartbreak.

Even so, it was hard to not get excited about the future. Despite everything that happened, Natalie would still love to be a Christmas bride. To have the church all decorated with poinsettias and trees with white lights illuminating the sanctuary. She stopped herself. No, that was the old Natalie. The one who believed in fairy tales and dream weddings. Not the Natalie who had to live in reality. That love doesn't always end with a kiss and sparklers.

"Natalie?"

The sound of a soft and familiar voice interrupted Natalie's daydream.

Natalie turned around to see Hannah, dressed in her scrubs, her hair pulled back in a neat ponytail, carrying a shopping bag.

"Hi," Natalie smiled. "I see you're busy getting some shopping done. Great minds think alike."

Hannah nodded. "Yes, I had some time after my shift ended and Ben has the kids for a fun outing before he flies out of town for a work trip tomorrow, so I figured I had better get started on some Christmas shopping. Did you just get here?"

Natalie pulled out a list from her purse. "I did. Trying to decide which store to go to first."

"I have some time if you'd like the company. It would be good to catch up."

Natalie nodded. "That would be great."

"What's on your Christmas list?" Natalie asked Hannah before she took a sip from her drink.

Hannah laughed. "To survive. Really, though these last few weeks of the year with all the kids' school projects and homework, the parties. It is so exhausting. I just pray we all stay healthy and well."

"I feel you. Some day it feels like I'm struggling to stay afloat."

"How is the festival planning coming along?"

Natalie paused. "There's definitely less interest this year." Thinking Hannah may have thought she was trying to recruit her to volunteer, she quickly added, "From the corporate sponsorships. So many businesses have shuttered this past year. I know it's been tough on all of us."

Hannah nodded in agreement. "Eli's mentioned a few things to me, but we don't talk about his work too much. I find it boring." As they left the toy store, they passed a department store with fancy dresses in the window. Natalie paused to look. Hannah stood next to her admiring the outfits.

"Do you have a dress for the Chamber dinner yet?"

Natalie shrugged. "I'm just going to wear a dress I already have. I don't go to fancy events like that very often, so I have a few standard dresses I always wear."

Hannah's eyes widened as she looked down at the price tag. "I know what you mean," She quickly released it before causing any damage.

"What are you getting Ben for Christmas?" Natalie asked, wondering whether she was going to get Eli something.

"Nothing," Hannah joked. "Well, not nothing. After the kids were born we decided to give each other an experience instead of stuff. All our clutter was making me very overwhelmed. Besides, neither one of us is very patient during the year, and if we want something we usually buy it ourselves," she answered.

"That is a good idea. I feel like I accumulate so much junk during the year. An experience is a great gift."

By the time Natalie and Hannah were done shopping, the store had begun to fill up with customers taking advantage of the Christmas sales. They found the checkout counter and got in line behind four people. Just as they were about to checkout, the customer in front of them shouted. "I want to see a manager!"

Natalie and Hannah looked at each other. Hannah rolled her eyes.

The cashier, who looked to be no more than fifteen or sixteen, turned beet red as she attempted to call her manager on the phone.

Growing increasingly impatient, the customer continued berating the cashier, "They used to have good customer service here," the man said as he turned to both Natalie and Hannah.

Natalie could feel her blood beginning to boil. She stepped forward.

"She is doing everything she can."

"Not fast enough," he argued.

"Sir, it's Christmas," Natalie said.

"So what?" he seethed.

Hannah motioned to Natalie that another register had opened up. Hannah and Natalie paid for their items and on their way out they saw the manager talking to the young cashier. Fighting back tears, the young cashier left the store and sat on a bench. Natalie went up to her.

"Hey, people can be such jerks can't they?"

The cashier nodded as a tiny tear broke through and slid down her face. Natalie opened her wallet and pulled out a five-dollar bill.

"Here, go get a cup of coffee before your next shift," she said.

"You don't have to do that," the young woman answered.

"Please. Merry Christmas," Natalie said with a smile.

The cashier lifted her head and smiled. "Thank you. Merry Christmas."

Natalie and Hannah continued walking.

"That was very sweet of you," Hannah answered.

"It was the least I could do. Retail workers take such a beating this time of year."

"They sure do. I worked at the mall when I was in high school and Black Friday through New Year's was the worst. People forget how to act in public. Common decency isn't too common anymore. It was astonishing to me. Especially as a sixteen-year-old. I think that's when I started losing some of the Christmas magic."

"You sound like Eli," Natalie joked.

"I'm not as bad as he is. He just avoids the holidays. Treats it as a vacation to go somewhere and avoid all the craziness I suppose. Especially since our parents died. He doesn't come out and talk about it very much, but I know that had something to do with it. For all of us really. Sometimes it's hard to make new memories when my heart keeps remembering the old ones. It just hurts."

As the words left Hannah, it felt like Natalie went back in time to her earlier daydream where she envisioned the church decorated for Christmas, the beautiful tall green tree draped with beautiful white tulle and silver ornaments. It was ready for a winter wedding, which she knew the church had every weekend in December. She could relate to the old memories popping up and how much they hurt. She tried not to dwell on them.

"I understand," Natalie said as they walked to the parking lot.

"What are you doing now? Do you want to come over to the house and wrap the presents and hang out?"

Natalie quickly thought through her afternoon schedule. She needed to work on a few projects for work, but could spare an hour or two. Sometimes friendships needed to take precedence over work and today was one of those days.

"Sure, that would be great."

Natalie put her gifts in the trunk and climbed in the front seat. Her favorite Christmas song came on the radio as she was pulling out of the parking lot. The perfect afternoon to refuel her soul.

Hannah dug out her gift wrap and fancy bows from the hall closet. The blue tub was filled to the top with an assortment of tissue paper, bows, and enough gift bags to give one to every child in Harbor Ridge. Twice. She and Natalie worked carefully and quickly to wrap the presents they brought at the mall.

"I love that you adopted two angels off the tree for the Salvation Army. I should start that tradition with Luke and Quinn. I feel like Christmas is a 'gimme' holiday to kids and this could teach them some compassion toward others," she said as she taped a fancy bow to the package.

"That's actually why I started doing the angel tree in the first place," Natalie said without looking up, unsure about whether she wanted to open up to Hannah.

"What do you mean?"

Natalie proceeded to tell Hannah about her almost wedding. About her heartbreak and how this time of year was so painful for her. To her surprise, Hannah didn't diminish her feelings. She sat and listened in solidarity.

"I'm sorry you went through all of that. The holidays are tough for me too. I miss my parents. A lot." Hannah seemed as though she might burst into tears at any moment, but she stopped herself, "But I want my kids to have a great Christmas, the same way my mom always made them so special for me. My mom collected Nativities. It seemed like there was one in every corner of the house when we were growing up. Eli would get into trouble by hiding the baby Jesus and replacing it with some kind of action figure." Natalie laughed so hard she snorted. Hannah smiled before laughing. Natalie's laugh was contagious.

"I could see Eli doing something like that."

"He tries to act all serious in his business but he can be a little mischievous."

Natalie remembered the weekend she was babysitting and how he came over to help. A smile emerged on her face. Eli definitely had his immature moments, but he could be sincere and sweet. Natalie turned her attention back to tying a bow on the package she bought to donate.

Natalie put her coat on and was about to open the front door when the doorbell rang. She opened it. Outside stood Hannah . . . wait, no. She was a little shorter, with longer hair tucked underneath a knit cap. Her eyes were frozen on Natalie.

"Hi, can I help you?" Natalie asked.

The young woman spoke so softly Natalie could barely hear her. "I must have the wrong address. I'm sorry to bother you." As soon as she arrived, the young woman turned away and headed for the stairs on the porch.

"Wait," Natalie answered as she followed her outside, "Who are you looking for?"

With the same whisper and her hands still nervously in her pockets, the young woman answered, "Hannah Hawkins?"

"You have the right house. I'm a friend of Hannah's. One minute," she said warmly.

Natalie waited for the young woman to say her own name, but when she didn't, she yelled for Hannah.

When Hannah came to the door, the color immediately drained from her face. She folded her arms in front of her chest as if to protect herself from any harm.

"This is my sister, Amy."

Chapter Eighteen

Hannah said it almost like a question. She turned back to Amy, "Look I don't know why you're here but we've all moved on. You've never answered anything I sent you and you think you can just show up on my doorstep and I'm going to let you in my house like we're some big happy family again? What do you want?"

"Let me explain. Please," Amy pleaded.

"You're four years too late," Hannah said as she walked back into the house leaving the door open.

Amy and Natalie's eyes met. Amy's eyes filled with tears before she rushed away quickly. Natalie felt pulled in both directions. She wanted to make sure both women were okay. She didn't know Amy, but Hannah's abruptness upset her. She had never seen Hannah treat anyone like that. It was shocking to her. Amy quickly disappeared. Natalie took a deep breath and walked back into the house to look for Hannah.

Natalie noticed Hannah hunched over on the couch. Unused gift wrap and ribbons strewn all over the floor. Her body shook with emotion as she held her face in her hands. Natalie sat down next to her.

Hannah took her hands down from her face revealing red eyes and messy mascara dripping down her cheeks. "I'm sorry you had to see that."

Natalie scooted the presents they had wrapped over and sat next to her and gave her a hug. Hannah's hug back felt weak.

Hannah sniffled. "I wasn't expecting to see her today. When our parents passed away, Amy had the choice to either stay with Hannah and finish high school or move out west and live with our aunt and uncle, her legal guardians until she turned eighteen. She decided to finish her senior year with them. Eli and I wanted her to stay here so we could all be together. She didn't want to and she left. We visited a few times early on but then life got busy and she didn't want to come back. Didn't want anything to do with us anymore." Hannah barely got out her words in a whisper.

It seemed as though the hurt was just as deep as it was when it first happened with how Hannah was acting. Hannah had kept her family a secret from Natalie for so long that when she opened up it was hard to stop.

"We found out my parents had passed away in an accident and my entire world shattered. I've never felt so broken in my life. We were all so close. Eli was working in another state. Amy still lived at home with them but she was over at a friend's house at the time. Ben and I would have taken her in to live with us. It was the summer before her senior year of high school. I had two toddlers. Ben worked all the time. I needed her and she abandoned us. I didn't just lose my parents. It felt like I lost my entire family."

"Amy's here now, maybe," Natalie started saying. Hannah raised her hand up in front of her face.

"No, she had her chance." Hannah stood up from the couch and walked into the kitchen.

Natalie sat still before standing up. She didn't know what to do. She decided it would be better to leave and give Hannah some space. As she left the house she noticed Ben pull up in the driveway. She quickly hopped in her car before he had the chance to talk to her. She didn't want to say the wrong thing again.

* * *

Hannah heard Ben come through the front door. She continued washing the dishes in the sink instead of greeting him as she usually did. She had been on the same plate the last five minutes. She turned to meet him as he entered the kitchen. She tried to put on a brave face, but Ben knew when something was off with her.

"You look like you've had a rough day," he said to Hannah, who was washing dishes at the sink.

"You could say that," she said, not looking up.

"What do you mean?" He put his hand gently on her shoulder.

Hannah turned to him, her eyes still bloodshot from crying, "Amy's back."

His mouth dropped, "What? Your sister Amy?" The words came slowly from his mouth.

"Yeah. She just came to the house and rang our doorbell, no call or text." Hannah scoffed, "So like her to do that. Inconsiderate as always." Hannah shook her head.

Ben wrapped his arms around Hannah's waist and pulled her closer "This is great news."

"Is it?" Hannah wondered aloud as she pulled away.

"Honey, you've been wanting to see and talk to her for four years and now she's back in Harbor Ridge. This is your chance to finally have closure. To finally talk."

Hannah sighed. She wasn't expecting to feel so angry. The years of silence had taken their toll and while she longed to go back to the years where she and Amy shared a room and secrets and even clothes sometimes, she wondered if it would ever be possible for her to forget about all the hurt she had caused their family. Or even more forgive her for walking away?

* * *

"I'm sorry, excuse me." Eli quickly reached in his pocket and turned the ringer off his phone. He had forgotten to put his phone on silent while he was in a meeting with a potential developer to build a new apartment complex in Harbor Ridge.

After his meeting, he went to his office where he closed the door. He called Hannah back, his heart beating quicker than it should. That was one of the unfortunate effects of getting a terrible phone call one day out of the blue. His antenna was up expecting there to be something wrong. He sat down at his desk as he waited for her to pick up.

He could barely make out her voice.

"Hannah, take a deep breath. What is wrong?"

He could hear her exhale through the phone. "Amy knocked on my door this afternoon. Four years and she couldn't make an effort other than a text here and there, but she decided to come to my house today."

Eli's stomach fell to the floor. Their sister was finally back around. Now it was his turn to exhale.

"How is she? Was she all right?" Eli rested his chin on his fist.

"She seemed like the same Amy." Hannah said dismissively.

Eli had so many questions. "Where is she staying? Is she staying with you?"

"What?" The volume in Hannah's voice made Eli pull the phone away from his ear. "No she's not staying with me. I didn't let her come in."

Eli paused and pulled on his tie. "I see. I don't know if Amy has my new number or not."

"I certainly haven't given it to her."

"Hannah, why did you call me? What is the plan?"

Eli heard silence on the other end of the line.

"There is no plan Eli. You can do whatever you want."

Eli ran his fingers through his hair and let out a sigh. "Hannah, don't put me in the middle of this. I hated that when we were kids."

"I never put you in the middle, that was always Amy. Mom and Dad always treated her differently because she was the baby of the family. If she thinks she can just walk back into my life without an apology or explanation then she doesn't know who she's dealing with. I don't have time for this right now."

Eli pulled the phone away from his head as she continued yelling. He shook his head. This was the exact kind of drama that he didn't need to be dealing with these last few weeks of his contract while he was trying to bring Harbor Ridge out of the red. He was already at more than the capacity of what he could handle emotionally dealing with Natalie. Now Hannah and Amy too. Still he was curious as to why Amy decided to come see Hannah. Why did she come back to Harbor Ridge?

Chapter Nineteen

Natalie walked into the welcome center at the church. She was looking forward to a morning of worship and getting back into a routine. Maybe that would make her feel like things were back to normal when it felt like anything but that. The week had been challenging to put it mildly and it would be nice to have the morning to reflect. To focus on something else besides her to do list that kept regenerating itself.

Sandy came up to Natalie before the service. "Matt is here with his *fiancé*," Sandy whispered. "Couldn't wait until Christmas Day like he had originally planned." Sandy shook her head.

"Matt got engaged? How are you doing with that?" Natalie said, sincerely happy for the couple.

"Well, it wouldn't have been my decision but here we are." Sandy sighed.

Just then Matt walked over with his new *fiancé*.

"Natalie, you know Matt and this is his *fiancé*, Amy," Sandy said, the words taking extra time coming out of her lips.

Natalie and Amy locked eyes. Natalie wasn't sure what to say. Out of habit, Natalie stuck out her hand. For a few moments neither of them spoke.

"Hi Amy, I'm Natalie, a friend of your future mother-in-law's" she nodded toward Sandy. "It's nice to meet you."

Natalie could see the relief in Amy's eyes that Natalie didn't bring up their meeting the day before. "Nice to meet you," Amy nodded as she shook her hand. Matt beamed at Amy. He had never looked happier.

Sandy interrupted, "We better go find our seats, the service will start soon. Join us for lunch after Natalie if you're free? Please." The last part sounded like a command from Sandy and not a question.

"Sure," Natalie nodded. Sandy was always so generous to treat Natalie to lunch on occasion and it would be nice to get to know Amy and catch up with Matt.

It seemed as though most of the church parishioners chose Antonio's Pizzeria as their lunch place too. The decor was dated but the food was reliable. It was always a mad dash after the later service to arrive before the other churches let out. The pizza buffet and salad bar gave everyone plenty of choices. Especially for those who had dietary needs, which Sandy mentioned more than a few times when she invited Natalie.

Natalie walked into the restaurant and saw Sandy sitting by the door.

"I'm so glad you could join us," Sandy said as she stood up to give Natalie a hug.

"Matt already got a table," she continued.

"And Amy?" Natalie questioned.

"Yeah, she's here too," Sandy said flatly. "It took us forever to decide on a place to eat. All of my opinions got vetoed."

Natalie ended up sitting in between Sandy and Amy. Amy and Matt spent most of the lunch making googly eyes at each other.

Natalie tried her best to cut the silence with questions to get to know Amy better. She hated sitting in silence, especially when it seemed their food was taking long.

"So Amy, what are you studying?" Natalie asked as she grabbed a roll from the bread basket across the table.

Amy looked at Matt. "Well I've had a few hiccups along the way getting my degree.

Sandy chimed in, "I graduated from college the same year I had Matt. Everyone has challenges. It's how we overcome them that matters."

Amy nodded shyly. Sandy stood up to return to the buffet. Natalie turned to Amy and whispered.

"It took me an extra semester to graduate too. Don't sweat it. Everyone is on their own timeline."

Amy smiled, "Thanks for telling me that. Sometimes I feel like such a failure."

"You're welcome and you are by no means a failure," Natalie smiled back warmly. She didn't know what had happened between Hannah and Amy all those years ago, but she was beginning to wonder if she had found a new friend.

After lunch and an unplanned post-lunch nap, Natalie gathered up enough energy to clean her apartment. She liked starting her week off fresh and getting rid of the clutter that somehow accumulated into Mount Everest in five days time. As she began to sift through her assorted papers she noticed her signed lease for the new year that she had forgotten to give Sandy at lunch. She decided to drop it off at Sandy's house on her way to the grocery store. She was about to drop the lease in the mailbox when she noticed Amy walking up the driveway. Amy waved at her.

"Hey," Amy said as she walked toward the car.

"Hi again. I need to drop something off for Sandy." She held up the manila envelope.

"Matt and his mom are still out shopping. I needed to get some fresh air and went for a run. Do you want to come in?" she asked.

Natalie had a million things on her to do list, but Amy's offer sounded inviting.

Amy opened the front door and then Natalie followed her in trying not to bump into the wreath hanging on the front door.

"Thanks for not acting awkward this morning. I know yesterday didn't go as well as I hoped it would with Hannah. I should have texted or called, but I'm much better at talking in person. Hannah and I don't exactly have a strong track record of communicating through texts." Amy smiled weakly. "I hope we can be friends. I need to make some friends, especially in Harbor Ridge."

"Why in Harbor Ridge?"

"Matt wants to move back after we get married. I still have a year left to finish but after that is done I'll move here and we'll be together." Amy smiled and then her expression turned more somber. "I should have called before I just showed up at Hannah's. She was really not happy to see me."

Natalie hesitated to get involved. "I think she was caught off guard. Hannah has a lot on her plate. We all do."

"I hope we can work things out. I guess I screwed that up when I moved away."

"You left?"

"Everything in this town reminded me of my dad and my mom. I couldn't go anywhere without the solemn looks and the questions about the accident or assumptions. Or how much everyone missed my parents. I know they meant well but it was exhausting. I was seventeen and just lost both my parents and my home. I needed to get away. I needed a fresh start. It was difficult but worth it. I met Matt and then his mom ended up retiring to the same town I grew up in. What are the odds?"

"So you knew it was time to return?"

"Yeah. I'm older now. Hopefully more mature. I know I hurt Hannah and Eli when I left but I had to do it, you know?"

Natalie understood more than she let on.

"I moved to Harbor Ridge to start over too. Sometimes we need a fresh start, right?"

"Yep. What brought you here?"

For some reason, Natalie felt like she should share her story with Amy. She thought if anyone could understand how she felt about a new beginning it would be Amy.

"I moved here a few years ago, I had a little bit of a personal crisis."

Amy nodded emphatically. "I know a little bit about one of those." Natalie smiled. She knew Amy and Hannah had their differences, but she couldn't help but feel for Amy. She took a deep breath and dove into her story.

"I was supposed to get married to my college sweetheart. We dated from freshman year through, well, December of our senior year. He proposed over Christmas break our junior year. We went ice skating and he set up a scavenger hunt on campus from all of the dates we'd been on throughout the three years we'd been dating. It was so romantic. He was everything I thought I ever wanted. I was so happy with him."

Natalie stopped. She could feel herself getting emotional all these years later.

"You don't have to tell me."

"No, it's silly. I don't know why I'm getting emotional. I'm over it," Natalie tried to reassure herself. She wiped away a tear that had snuck out with her pinky.

"Anyways, we set a date for the year after we got engaged. I had the dress, the shoes, a deposit down for the caterer, the church, everything was taken care of. I was so excited about being a Christmas bride."

She smiled. Well, a half-smile. She could still see it in her head. The way the church would have been decorated. The way she felt the first time she tried on her wedding dress. Her mom's wedding veil she wanted to wear. She caught herself. That dream had died. And if she was being honest with herself, it felt like part of herself had died that day too.

"We sent out wedding invitations—they were so beautiful. White with silver snowflakes in the background. I don't know if that's what spooked him or not, but a week after the invitations went out, just as people started receiving them, my fiancé—well ex-fiancé—told me he didn't want to get married anymore."

There weren't many people in Harbor Ridge who knew this part of Natalie's story and she preferred to keep it that way. She hated the questions and assumptions. The comparisons. Or her least favorite, when they knew someone who had their heart broken but had found love again. She wasn't there yet and couldn't see herself with anyone. Couldn't see herself trusting again.

Amy's eyes widened. "Wow. That is crazy. So you left too?"

"I was so heartbroken, I didn't even finish exams that year. I transferred colleges the very next semester. I did not want to see my ex-fiancé everyday. I couldn't be on the same campus that held such hard memories. We had planned on going to graduate school together and I had to regroup on what my plans were going to be. Some of my credits didn't transfer and I had to go to an extra semester of college but it was worth it to just be away from everything." So many of *their* dreams had been *his* dreams. She wasn't sure she knew what her dreams were anymore.

"Do you have any contact with the guy? What is he doing now?"

Natalie pondered. It was a question she had honestly not thought much about in a while. Some of her friends had thought there had to be somebody else he was dating for how sudden he had broken off things. It was too painful for Natalie to even go there. What difference did it make? It hurt just the same.

"I honestly don't know. Mentally I had to cut ties with him to avoid all the what-ifs. I didn't want to live in the past." Some days it felt like she still did.

Natalie wasn't sure she'd ever have closure on what happened and if she'd ever get a straight answer as to why he broke up with her.

Amy turned back to her.

"I need your help. You know Hannah and Eli. You know them better than I do right now. They trust you. Can you please try and convince them to talk to me? It's important." Amy's eyes looked down at the floor. "I know I shouldn't have left the way I did, but I'm back now. I want to connect with them again. I promised Matt I would try."

"I can't make you any promises, but I'll do my best," Natalie shrugged.

"Thank you!" Amy's eyes lit up for the first time Natalie had met her. She reached out her hands.

Natalie wondered if she was getting Amy's hopes up for nothing. Eli would be easier to convince than Hannah, she thought.

Chapter Twenty

The pile of not-good-enough dresses was growing as Natalie struggled to settle on the perfect dress for the Chamber dinner. Natalie thought her standard cocktail dress would do, but she had second thoughts and dug through her closet to find another. She should have decided before now. Maybe she didn't because she wasn't sure the night would even happen. Natalie pulled the green sparkly dress off the hanger and slowly put it on. This was the one.

She spent the morning painting her toenails and fingernails. She thought about making an appointment at a nail salon but couldn't make it work with her budget. After scouring the internet for a video to show her how to do the perfect up-do, Natalie felt pleased with how it turned out.

Her phone buzzed with a text that he was on his way and her face flushed. She peeked out of her second story window with anticipation just as Eli was pulling up to her apartment. Eli walked to Natalie's door. He knocked gently announcing his arrival.

She glanced one last time at the mirror before she opened the door revealing her dark green gown. A silver brooch brought together the ruching. Her hair, loose around her shoulders, curled at the bottom.

Eli couldn't stop staring at her.

"What?" she asked nervously as they walked out to his car. Her knees wobbled as she took his hand and walked the short distance to her car.

"You are beautiful," he smiled as he leaned forward to kiss her forehead before opening the passenger door for her. The kiss sent butterflies from her forehead to her toes. Natalie wondered if he would try to kiss her before the evening was over. She wouldn't stop him if he tried. He felt safe to her and for the first time she was ready to put her heart out there. He would protect it.

Natalie slowly sat into the passenger seat before turning her heels into the car on the freshly vacuumed floorboard. She pulled her gown into the car. So much dress. She reached to turn on the holiday radio station and started humming along. Eli sat down in the driver's seat and promptly turned down the volume.

"I think there'll be plenty of Christmas music at the party, don't you?"

"There's no such thing as too much Christmas music," Natalie joked. Eli winced. The smell of his aftershave filled the car tickling Natalie's nose.

They pulled up to the convention center where the party was going to be held. Eli handed the keys to the valet who took and parked the car. The white columns were wrapped in garlands and white lights that twinkled in the dark night. Eli grabbed Natalie's hand and they walked into the grand hall passing the elaborate decorations. The warmth from his hand made Natalie take off her jacket. After making some small talk with a few of Eli's coworkers, they found their assigned table.

"So is this your date?" One of Eli's coworkers asked. "This is my friend, Natalie," Eli corrected him as he took a sip of water from his glass.

Friend, Natalie thought. Of course, Eli didn't date between Halloween and Valentine's Day, she had been kidding herself if she thought she of all people could get Eli Collins to like her.

She noticed Eli hadn't come back from the buffet line and saw him talking to the mayor of Harbor Ridge in the corner of the ballroom. It looked serious. She wondered if Eli would clue her in later. Dinner went by rather quickly as Natalie took in the conversation from the other people at the table. There were two extroverts who seemed to be competing on who had the better winter vacation planned. Each sentence added to the one upping of the other. The whole conversation both annoyed and amused Natalie.

Eli made a joke that had the whole table laughing. She almost didn't notice when Eli stood up from his chair. He leaned down and whispered in her ear.

"Would you like me to bring you back something from the dessert table?"

"I would rather pick it out myself. " She laughed as she stood up to join him.

He smiled back at her and waited as she pushed back her chair and stood up. He put his hand on her lower back as they walked along the perimeter of the ballroom weaving between tables and wait staff. When they finally arrived at the buffet line, there were at least a dozen people in front of them.

"I ran into your sister Amy yesterday," Natalie said.

Eli slowly turned and looked at her. His eyes widened.

"I think if you'd talk to her you'd see that she's being sincere. She's trying," Natalie said hopefully.

"I really don't want to get into this tonight. Hannah and I aren't ready to talk to her yet. Please don't get involved. It's complicated." Eli turned and followed in line at the dessert table. Natalie rushed to catch up with him.

"I never asked to be involved. I just happened to be over at Hannah's when she came back. She just happens to be engaged to the son of one of my good friends."

Shock took over Eli's face. "Amy's engaged? How do you know that? Why do you know this?"

Natalie put her hand over her mouth and sighed. "You didn't know?"

Eli shook his head, "I told you. It's complicated. So that's why she came back. Probably wants money or something. She always has an agenda."

"You don't know that."

Eli stepped toward her. "And you think you do. You think you know everything about her. Everything about *my* family?"

Natalie took offense to his comment. "I've spent more time with Hannah than you the past few years." She mumbled, "I guess Amy, too."

She glanced from the floor to his eyes. His expression was filled with hurt and anger. She couldn't help herself.

"You don't think Amy was scared to come to Harbor Ridge? She wants to have a relationship with you and Hannah and the kids. She asked me if I could get you to talk to her. To just talk to her. Why is it so hard for you to forgive her? She's your sister."

Eli stopped, his back still turned from Natalie. He slowly turned around. Their eyes met. Eli scrunched his forehead.

"Why is it so hard for you to mind your own business? Our drama doesn't concern you. You're not our family," he spewed. He crossed his arms and his whispered voice became louder. "Maybe if you spent less time trying to make Hannah's family *your* family and started putting yourself out there, you could find your own."

Natalie felt her stomach fall to her overpriced black pumps. "What?" she whispered, in disbelief that he would bring up something so hurtful to change the subject.

"You're so busy taking care of Luke and Quinn and getting involved in other things that do not concern you. You want Hannah's life . . . that promotion at the hospital you told me you wanted but, 'don't have time for.'" He used air quotes to emphasize his point which further annoyed Natalie. He looked back at her "Or is it that you're not making time for it?"

Natalie could feel the tears starting to burn her eyes but she was determined to not break his stare. She didn't move when a single tear leaked out from her left eye. Eli's eyes narrowed.

"Not so fun when someone else tries to tell you how to live your life, is it?"

Natalie tried to open her lips to respond but she couldn't muster the strength. Natalie felt like she did in first grade when she fell off the monkey bars and got the wind knocked out of her. So stunned at his accusation, she could barely breathe. This was not the Eli she thought she knew.

After what seemed like an eternity, Natalie slowly turned and walked away. She rushed to the front door of the ballroom, but on her way she passed a table where a lady was eating what looked to be a delicious chocolate cheesecake with fresh strawberries on top. She quickly made a beeline for the dessert table, determined to not let the dinner go completely to waste. While she waited for the caterer to put her cheesecake in a to-go container, she pulled out her phone to order an Uber, her hands still shaking as she put in her information.

She quickly walked past the decorations, not stopping to look or admire them this time. Hoping, praying that her ride would get there soon and she could go back to her apartment. Back to where she could be alone. Back to where she would be safe. She pushed the doors open and a big gush of wind sent a chill through her.

Natalie crossed her arms and shivered while she waited for her Uber to show up. Five more minutes, her app displayed. She turned and saw Eli walking down the hallway in a hurry and quickly turned around hoping he didn't see her. She had no interest in ever talking to him again.

The Uber app dinged letting her know that her ride had arrived. She quickly opened the door to the car and slid into the backseat carefully pulling the bottom of the dress into the car. The driver, a young man, attempted to make small talk.

"Early evening?"

"Obviously," she mumbled.

The car ride home brought on a wave of nausea. She felt every bump on the road. Replaying their conversation in her head. Eli's words hurt worse with each rehashing of the night. She was grateful she was able to pay the fare with the app on her phone. She had forgotten to bring along her wallet, thinking she wouldn't be needing it.

Once home she changed out of her dress into her comfy pajamas and was relieved to take off her uncomfortable shoes. She took off her makeup, taking extra care to clean off the dried mascara from her face.

She leaned over the sink as more tears snuck out. This is why she didn't put herself out there. She felt so sad, she was almost nauseous. The pain of getting her hopes up for a date she had been waiting for, for so long was immense. She replayed their conversation in her head wishing she had never brought up Amy. Wondering what would have happened if she hadn't? She let out a deep breath. It would have come out eventually when Eli found out that Matt and Amy were engaged, and that Natalie knew about it.

"Always the pumpkin, never the princess," she mumbled to herself as she put on her pajamas. Maybe Eli was right about Christmas. Maybe the magic has an expiration date. Her tree sparkled in the corner of her apartment. She yanked the cord out of the wall, dimming the apartment.

She turned on the television and found a news station and despite everything that was on her mind, she fell asleep on the couch.

Her phone dinged, waking her up. Groggy, she sat up on the couch and stood up to get her phone. She turned on the lamp, giving light to her dark apartment. *11:15 p.m.*

1 wanted to make sure you got home okay. I spent an hour looking for you. I don't like picking you up and then not taking you home. Call me.

Natalie tossed her phone to the other side of the couch. If he had wanted to make sure she got home okay, he should have been the one to take her home. She re-read his message slowly. No apology offered in it either and she was in no mood to continue their conversation. She silenced her phone and plugged it in.

She slowly walked to her bedroom passing her dress and dancing shoes on the couch, that never got the chance to make it on the dance floor.

* * *

Eli stood in front of the bathroom mirror. He carefully took out his contacts, putting them in the gray and blue case and then washed his face and brushed his teeth before putting on his glasses. He quickly touched the screen of his phone to make sure he hadn't missed a reply from Natalie. For a second he thought maybe the sound was off and she could have texted him back.

No response, yet at least. His stomach flipped over when he thought about how the night had gone. It was so far from his expectations of when the night started. He had lost his temper. Plain and simple. He had not expected the mayor to corner him like that and talk about how the city was still struggling. Decades of decline in revenue and residents leaving the area and Eli was supposed to fix it all in a few months.

Healing took time.

When he closed his eyes he could still picture the way Natalie looked in that green dress when she first opened the door, the way her nose scrunched when she laughed at one of his jokes. His pulse raced when he thought about how his words had hurt her. It was like she shriveled up right in front of him.

She had no right to intervene in his family's life though. She didn't know everything that happened the past few years and who was she to judge him or Hannah for taking their time to forgive Amy. She wasn't there when Amy said all those hurtful things. So had he and Hannah. Grief makes people do weird things.

It was easier to point out Natalie's shortcomings than take responsibility of his own. Easier to pretend that Amy was the problem. Instead of acknowledging his silence played a part too. Lazy of him really. Besides, it wasn't like Natalie had gotten past whatever it was in her life that took her confidence or self-esteem. If she had, she was doing a lousy job of moving on from it. Eli wished Natalie could move on with him. Eli wanted to date again, but the thought of going through such a bad breakup again made him weary of even trying. Natalie began to change his thinking on that. Or at least she had.

He spent the last few years pouring his time into his position and traveling to new cities every few months, he had forgotten what it felt like to feel butterflies again. What it felt like to want to see someone everyday and even then not having enough time together.

He hated feeling the pain of losing her. They hadn't even had the chance to start. How would they ever begin a relationship if she wouldn't respond to his text? He briefly thought about going to her townhouse and knocking on the door to make sure she got home safely but he wasn't sure she wanted to see him. He didn't know what to say to her either. Part of him knew he went too far. He could tell by the look on her face when he suggested she'd been making excuses for where she was in life. He regretted the words almost immediately as he said them. Not because they weren't true, but because they were said in the heat of the moment. It wasn't what he said but how he said it.

Natalie was capable of so much if only she could see herself from his perspective. She was whip smart and creative. Her work ethic was strong and the way she was with children was something special to watch. For a moment, Eli thought if by some chance being a dad turned out to be in the cards for him, it would be hard to find a better mother than Natalie.

He brought his phone cord in from the kitchen and plugged it in next to his nightstand. He was hoping his phone would ding before he went to sleep. He tossed and turned for a while before finally falling asleep. No response came.

Chapter Twenty-One

Natalie overslept her alarm. She had spent all night replaying the evening with Eli over and over again in her head. She missed the special orchestra concert that morning at church and spent the rest of Sunday moping around in her pajamas. She needed to go to the grocery store and get food for the week, but even that simple task seemed too much. She wondered what Eli was up to. She let herself daydream about that Sunday he surprised her in the donut room after her solo in the cantata.

Usually listening to a festive and upbeat Christmas song could get her in a good mood, but today nothing seemed to work. Natalie was ready for Christmas to be over and onto the New Year. A time to start over and begin a new season. At least she still had the Live Nativity and Festival to look forward to.

A smile came across her face for the first time as she pictured the angel choir leading the way to the manger scene. It was her favorite part of the entire evening. The lights were dimmed before the choir sang "Joy to the World" a cappella. It wasn't long before the entire audience joined in unison. It was hard to not get pulled into the singing. From the great-grandparents to the littlest participants, there was a real feeling of togetherness and of hope. Natalie couldn't wait. She needed it this year. As much, if not more, as she did that first year she joined.

By the time Monday rolled around the following morning, she was ready for her routine and the distraction of work to keep her mind occupied. She slept a little better than the night before, but was still grateful there was fresh coffee in the breakroom. Natalie quietly slid into her office chair and sipped on her coffee while she waited for her computer to boot up.

"How was your weekend?" Rachel asked as her head peeked over the cubicle.

"Nothing special," Natalie kept typing.

"I saw you from a distance at the Chamber dinner with a very good-looking date. Is he the reason you bailed on our table?" Rachel walked around to Natalie's desk.

"Unfortunately." Natalie's head was still buried in her computer.

Rachel twisted her pen in her hair as she continued to pepper questions. "Who was he? Someone you met on the app? Is he the fun uncle? Hannah's brother?"

Natalie couldn't ignore her any longer and looked up.

"He's no one," she announced emphatically. So much for working being a distraction. Natalie turned back to her computer monitor and began typing aggressively, hoping it would send a message to Rachel.

But Rachel continued with her questions. "Just in the friend zone? So is he available?"

Natalie looked up and sighed. "I don't think we're going to be friends either."

Rachel pouted her lips. "I'm sorry. Dating is so weird these days. I'm on four different apps and *still* can't find a good one."

Natalie didn't even acknowledge Rachel's last comment. She meant well and was trying to help Natalie, but Natalie wasn't in the mood to be on the rebound. Whatever it was or wasn't between her and Eli was over. Gone before it even started. She opened her email inbox and noticed a new email from Linda Mueller. It was official. Linda was retiring, effective Dec. 31st.

Out of the corner of her eye, she noticed Linda walking toward her desk. Natalie quickly tidied up her workspace. Linda walked around to Natalie's cubicle. Natalie rotated in her office chair to meet Linda face to face.

"Natalie, do you have a few minutes for us to talk in my office?"

She immediately thought Linda was going to fire her. Usually when Linda called her into a meeting it was to correct something Natalie had done on an assignment.

"Natalie, you may have heard some rumors, but I wanted to let you know that I am retiring at the end of the year. Human Resources is doing an internal search to fill my position first and if there are no candidates, they will be posting it online next week."

Linda's voice got quieter as she leaned down to Natalie. "I told Jeff that he should keep his eyes out for your resume. You've gone above and beyond these last two and a half years proving yourself again and again with each event that's been placed in your lap. You should apply and I will be disappointed if you don't ask me to be a reference."

Natalie took a deep breath. She was not being fired. She laughed at herself. Always catastrophizing for no reason.

Natalie walked back to their desk. Rachel slid her chair back over.

"What was that about?"

"We were right. Linda is retiring. She told me I should apply as her replacement." The last sentence came out slow from Natalie's mouth. It wasn't a shock that Linda was retiring. She had been showing signs of that for weeks. Natalie wasn't sure whether she was ready to tackle Linda's role. It gave her a confidence boost that Linda thought she could handle the job. Proof that Natalie's hard work hadn't gone unnoticed or unappreciated. After the last week she had, Linda's confidence in her ability made her feel great.

"You should go for it," Rachel reassured her.

Rache's confidence meant everything to her. "Maybe I will."

Natalie swiveled back to her desk and clicked on the attachment to Linda's email. She slowly read through each line. The position would be full-time hours with benefits. If she got the job she would be overseeing the entire group of volunteers as well as managing all new volunteer orientations. It had always been a dream of Natalie's to move up. What if she applied and didn't get it and then had to work next to the person who beat her for the position every day? Would she feel rejected every day like she had for the last four years? Not good enough?

She replayed Eli's conversation in her head. It was as if he was standing next to her repeating the same conversation that she was shortchanging herself. Maybe she was? Maybe she had been? Eli was wrong about one thing, though. She didn't want Hannah's family. No, she desperately wanted her own. She wanted her own job and family, but she was scared to put herself out there. Her confidence has taken a beating the last few years. But who's permission was she waiting on?

What had playing it safe gotten her the last few years? Sure she had been coasting through an easy job at the hospital and filling her time with babysitting and volunteering with the kids at church but she was ready for more. She responded to Linda's email thanking her for sending the job application and telling her she was going to apply. After she clicked send on the email, a rush of nervous excitement rushed through her. Now there was no turning back. If she promised Linda she was going to do something, she better deliver.

She then moved her focus to the Festival of Trees vendor reports on who had outstanding debts to pay. She glanced up at the clock and sighed after noticing she was only forty-five minutes into her shift. It was going to be a long day, but at least she had a stack of files to work through.

Natalie sat on her couch watching one of her murder mystery shows. She wasn't in the mood for one of those Christmas movies. Eli was right, they were cheesy, and when did life ever end up tied up in a perfect bow with a kiss under the mistletoe and snow falling in the background? Case in point: they were supposed to be at the townhouse complex's movie night showing of *Elf* together. Sandy put on a Christmas party every year for the tenants of her building. She ran into Sandy on her way home who was setting up the area. Natalie made some excuse for why she decided not to go.

That night at home, with her heart continuing to beat heavy, Natalie worked on her resume. She hadn't updated it in three years. She typed out her cover letter before clicking *submit*. Almost immediately she had second thoughts and wished she could have retracted her application.

Being brave was new to Natalie. Yet as each minute ticked by Natalie felt more at peace with putting herself out there. What did she have to lose?

Chapter Twenty-Two

Eli sat at his desk typing his report to the present to the board. There was no good solution for what they asked him to do, but with input from their finance chairwoman, he felt confident in suggesting a one percent tax increase or canceling the discretionary spending the city had planned. People liked choices and he knew letting them make the decision took it out of his hands. His job was to provide the information to guide their decision but ultimately leave it in their hands.

Eli stayed at the office past seven o'clock that evening. His weekend had not been productive and he needed to finish his contract out strong before his next assignment. A few of his coworkers asked him what happened to his date who didn't return to their table and he made up some excuse that she hadn't felt good and had to leave. What else could he have said? He still felt like the biggest jerk for snapping at her the way he did.

Eli texted Hannah about bringing Luke's soccer cleats over to their house tonight, but he had forgotten it was the night of Ben's office holiday party. Natalie was babysitting. Eli had to make up some excuse why he couldn't stop by. He told Hannah he was swamped at work, which wasn't a total lie. Work had definitely picked up. He was used to making work the most important thing in his life. He would work as long as he wanted to.

Maybe he should move on? It wasn't too much longer that he would be onto his next contract. Next month, he'd been skiing with his single buddies in Colorado enjoying himself and forgetting about Harbor Ridge again.

Why did every moment make him think of her? They couldn't end things like this. At least he hoped not.

Chapter Twenty-Three

Hannah had been smiling all day. Ben's company was having their annual Christmas party and Hannah was finally going to be able to attend one with him. All week she was holding her breath that one of the kids didn't come home with an illness from school. Why did it seem like someone was constantly ill during these cold and bleak winter months? It seemed as though every year something got in the way of her attending; the kids were sick, the weather was awful, or their babysitter canceled at the last minute.

Not this year, she prayed.

Hannah had bought a new dress, made her first hair appointment in ages, and was looking forward to getting all dolled up. She was thankful Natalie had agreed to babysit, and was especially grateful to have the distraction from even thinking about Amy. It was easier to pretend everything was okay. Easier to not think about it at all.

The doorbell rang and Ben went to answer it while Hannah put the finishing touches on her makeup. She couldn't remember the last time she felt this beautiful. Most days, she rushed out of the house with barely enough time to eat breakfast and toss her hair back in a hair tie. She had forgotten what it felt like to spend time getting ready, to spend time on herself for a change.

She heard a whistle coming from outside her bathroom. She looked up and saw Ben, dressed to the nines, in a tuxedo. A little too much aftershave, but she'd take it.

He moved in closer and kissed her slowly. "Wow, you look stunning."

"Thank you. You cleaned up pretty well yourself," she added.

Hannah came downstairs while the kids were eating dinner. Quinn sat next to them holding a green cup of water.

"Wow, Mommy! You look so beautiful. Like a princess," Quinn exclaimed. She scooted her chair out from behind the table and rushed over to give her mom a hug.

"You look great, I love your dress." Natalie said.

"Thank you, I don't get the chance to get dressed up and go out too often so I splurged a little on it," she said.

"Doesn't she look great?" Ben said as he walked into the kitchen giving Hannah a kiss.

Luke covered his eyes, "Eww!"

Hannah laughed.

"Now you both be on your best behavior for Natalie," she said before turning to Natalie.

"We should be home by eleven. The kids can stay up until eight tonight but I know they want to go to church tomorrow so they need to get their rest."

"Of course, I will have them in bed at the usual time. Have a great time!"

"Thanks," Ben said as he and Hannah walked to the front door.

"Help yourself to anything you want while we're gone."

"Thank you. I'm just not that hungry tonight. I had a big lunch at work."

"Can we play Candy Land?" Quinn asked as she finished her slice of pizza.

"Of course, I know it's your favorite," Natalie answered.

"But I wanted to play Battleship," Luke argued.

"How about we play Candy Land first and then we play Battleship after," Natalie said as she kneeled down to his eye level reassuring him that he would get a chance to play a game too.

Hannah loved the way Natalie treated her children. It was though Natalie didn't see them as little kids but like young adults in the making. In typical

Natalie fashion, she came with activities for the kids.

Hannah felt herself relax. Quinn and Luke were in good hands. Ben and Hannah walked hand in hand to his car. He opened the passenger side door for her. She looked up at him and put her arms around him.

"I can't believe I finally get to go to one of your company's Christmas parties," she said.

"I know. It'll be fun!" He gently pushed a stray hair behind her ear as he caressed her cheek and lowered his lips to hers. His kiss took her breath away and while years ago she had thought it might be the end for them, their hard work on their marriage had paid off. Better than ever. Hannah pulled away and smiled. She slid into the passenger seat as Ben slowly closed the car door.

As they drove down the road toward the restaurant where the Christmas party was taking place, Hannah held Ben's hand that was resting on the center console.

"Let's make a point of going on more dates. I know we say it at the beginning of every year, but I need you. I need us, our time," Hannah said.

"I couldn't agree more. I know I've been caught up with work and our schedules haven't aligned since you went back to work but I will try to make more of an effort, I promise."

"I will too. I love you so much," Ben whispered in her ear as he leaned across the console.

"I love you too," as she went in for another kiss.

* * *

Natalie sat at the kitchen table across from Quinn and Luke who were covered in a mixture of green and red glitter and white glue. She had not wanted to come but canceling would have been unfair to Hannah. Selfish like Eli. Gah, she couldn't get him out of her head.

"Oh I love it! Can we go hang it on the tree right now?" Quinn asked eagerly as she held up an ornament she had finished decorating with glitter. There was more glitter than ornament.

Natalie gently took it from Quinn's hands. "We should let it dry first. It looks beautiful."

Quinn beamed as Natalie laid down her ornament on the table to dry.

"I don't want to wait. I want to put it on the tree *now*." Quinn picked it up. The ornament fell apart. Quinn began to cry.

Natalie sighed. "I'm sorry it broke. Sometimes we have to wait. I know it's hard to be patient. Why don't we go do something else while we wait for yours to dry?"

Quinn stood up from the table and clapped her hands. "Ooh! Can we make cookies?"

Luke set down the book he was looking at. "Uncle Eli makes the best cookies. Can he come over? Like last time?"

Natalie looked down at both their smiling faces. She didn't know her heart could break again, but it did. She took a deep breath and changed the subject. "How about another craft or a game?"

They both nodded and were fine to put baking cookies off until another time. Thankfully she was off the hook.

Natalie thought of how she used to have that childlike enthusiasm about Christmas. The older she got and the more responsibilities she had, the easier it was to lose sight of the joy.

"Do you want to make one?" Quinn asked.

Natalie hesitated. Quinn's eyes sparkled.

"Sure, let's do it together."

* * *

Ben carefully put his suit jacket over Hannah's shoulders as she slowly walked to the valet station. If it wasn't twenty degrees outside she would have walked there barefoot. Her feet were killing her. So much dancing and such delicious food that she didn't have to cook or share, the evening quickly flew by as they enjoyed an uninterrupted four-course dinner. It was close to eleven when they finally pulled into their driveway. The house was dark except for a lamp left on. Natalie sat next to it on the couch, reading a book she had gotten from the library. She stood up to greet them. "How was it?"

Hannah felt a smile emerge on her face. "It was perfect. Thank you again for watching the kids. I hope they behaved for you."

"They were great as usual. I've enjoyed getting to be their babysitter."

"Bedtime go okay?"

Natalie laughed. "A little stalling but nothing out of the ordinary." It was predictable.

"Great. I'll venmo you for tonight." As Hannah opened the drawer in the kitchen, she turned back to Natalie. "I've been meaning to ask how was the Chamber dinner? I've been so busy this week I didn't get a chance to talk to Eli."

She looked up and saw Natalie's expression change. She was not expecting that.

"Oh, um . . . yeah, I ended up leaving early," Natalie said softly.

Hannah was confused. She knew how much Eli had been looking forward to it. And Natalie, too, or at least she'd thought. "Did you get sick or something?"

"Not exactly, but there's something I need to talk to you about."

A sense of dread came over Hannah. This was not going to be good news.

Chapter Twenty-Four

Eli paused to take a sip of coffee. This was his fourth cup of the day and it was barely ten a.m. With the end of the year coming up along with his contract, he was busy. He slowly turned his neck at the sound of his office door opening.

Before he could fully turn around he heard his sister's voice exclaim, "What did you do?"

Startled, Eli nearly dropped his coffee cup.

"What are you doing here?"

Hannah dropped her purse on the only part of Eli's desk that wasn't occupied by a manila folder and put her hands on her hips as she looked at him with frustration. "Natalie gave her notice. She's no longer going to be able to babysit. Said she needed some space." She shrugged. "And you didn't respond to any of my texts. That's not like you."

"Well yeah. Things are kinda busy right now." He motioned to his cluttered desk. Hannah didn't seem to get the message.

She raised her eyebrow. "She just happens to quit the weekend after you take her to the Chamber party?"

"Why are you yelling at me? How is this my fault?"

He'd tried reaching out to Natalie and she hadn't responded. It was out of his hands. He didn't have the energy or the time to devote to this drama. He was not about to chase after some girl, woman, whatever who did not want to be chased.

Not satisfied with Eli's silence, Hannah continued, "I know you and Natalie didn't leave the Chamber dinner together."

Eli shifted the papers on his desk and reached for his mug to take a sip. Hannah continued, "I was on my lunch break yesterday and overheard the admin team talking about how she left the party early. At eight o'clock if I recall."

"You *overheard* or you went on a fishing expedition? Fishing for gossip?"

Hannah folded her arms in front of her chest. "That's not the point. It doesn't matter how I got the information just that I know now."

Eli folded his arms and shook his head. "Right, I forgot, can't keep anything a secret in this town. Hopefully I won't be here too much longer."

Hannah walked over to his desk. "Why would you say that? We've loved having you in Harbor Ridge and getting to be a part of our lives. The kids especially have."

The corner of Eli's mouth drew up slightly. Being an uncle was the best part of getting to live in Harbor Ridge again. Hannah took a more serious tone.

"I wish you would have listened to me about not getting involved with Natalie. I was worried this was going to happen."

"What was going to happen?"

"Oh come on Eli, you haven't had a real relationship since Kendra, and we lost Mom and Dad. I want that for you, but I'm not sure that's what you want."

"I don't know what I want. But it's certainly not someone telling me what to do all the time." He half-smiled as he elbowed Hannah. "I get enough of that from you."

"Please make it right. What happened?"

"Not that this is any of your business, but she was trying to insert herself where she didn't belong. Not unlike this situation."

"So go see her in person. Figure it out."

He motioned to the pile of paperwork overtaking one corner of his desk. "We'll see. I've got a lot going on."

Betty, Eli's administrative assistant, knocked quietly on his office door. Hannah waved goodbye to Eli as she quickly left his office. Betty walked over to Eli's desk and handed him another folder to add to the pile.

"Bryan is out sick for the remainder of the week with the flu so you're going to need to sign off on the rest of the budget. She turned and walked away.

"Thank you."

Eli opened the folder and saw the notes on which cuts were being made. He closed the folder and sighed before angrily tossing it on his desk. His recommendations had not been considered.

* * *

Matt and Sandy were playing checkers at their kitchen table. It seated eight, and for many years Sandy dreamed about the day it would be filled. Life hadn't quite turned out the way she expected it to. When Matt's dad had left, she was in her early thirties and she had envisioned getting remarried some day, but it hadn't happened. She didn't want Matt rushing into a relationship like she had. Sandy's hands cupped around a snowman mug filled with warm hot tea and honey. She took a sip.

"I'm just surprised, that's all. I figured if you were going to propose to Amy, you would have told me beforehand instead of ambushing me. I thought you would have let me in."

Matt shook her head, knocking some of his hair over his eyes. "Ambush? I tried telling you about her and us when I would call you, but you always changed the subject. You don't want me to get married. Not just to Amy, but not at all."

"I never said that."

Matt pushed his chair back and stood up from the table.

"You didn't have to. I can tell by the way you treat her. Everything is so tense in this house. You would rather me say I don't want to get married."

"That's up to you."

In frustration Matt sternly said, "I don't want to get married."

Sandy looked up from the table, to see Amy directly behind Matt. Amy dropped the grocery bags she had been holding. The sound of the side door shutting came soon after.

Sandy's and Matt's eyes met.

"I have to go after her."

Sandy nodded.

Her phone rang. She looked at the screen, intrigued by the number of the person calling, but let it go to voicemail. She was in no mood to talk with anyone.

She walked to the front of the house and sat down in her chair. This was not the Christmas she had hoped to have, not the Christmas she was expecting. She pushed back on the recliner and elevated her feet. How did things become such a mess?

* * *

Matt wished he was wearing shoes instead of bedroom slippers as he rushed after Amy, but he had to catch up with her. He had to explain what she thought she had heard. As he got closer to her, he shouted.

"Amy, would you stop walking? Amy!"

He got no response or acknowledgment.

Matt shivered as he caught up to her. She turned and walked in a new direction on the sidewalk. He quickly stepped in front of her forcing her to stop. She looked up at him, her eyes a mixture of sadness and anger.

"Amy, your lips are turning blue. Please come inside."

Amy shook her head as she softly spoke. "My own family doesn't want anything to do with me, and now after not only flying across the country, but deciding to spend Christmas with you and your mom over my aunt and uncle, I find out you don't want me either. The only reason I'm even in

Harbor Ridge is because of you."

Matt took a step toward her and put his hand on her shoulder which she promptly shrugged off.

"Of course I want you. I asked you to marry me, didn't I?"

"Then why did you say that to your mom?" She lifted her head up and her eyes looked right through him. "I heard you. You said, 'I don't want to get married.'"

"I was just repeating what I thought she wanted me to say. I do want to marry you. I just . . ."

"Just what?"

Matt didn't know what to say. He needed more time. Amy kept walking as he stared at her as she walked away.

* * *

Sandy heard the front door slam and as she walked over to the staircase from the kitchen, she saw the back of Matt's brown hair as he turned at the top of the stairs.

"Matt?"

He stopped and shook his head, refusing to turn around and make eye contact. He continued to his room and she heard his door slam.

Her stomach rose to her chest. How was this the way her Christmas was turning out? The last Christmas before Matt would be getting a job, and who knew what his vacation schedule would be like then? Who knew if he'd ever come home after Christmas after this year? Would he be with Amy's family? Maybe she'd be spending next Christmas alone. She'd have no one to blame but herself.

Her phone rang again taking her out of her rabbit hole of despair. She walked back into the kitchen trying to remember where she left it. She followed its muffled ding and found it under a wadded-up tea towel that Matt had forgotten to hang back up. She picked up her cell phone and dialed the number back from her missed call.

"Hi Mayor Ethridge, this actually isn't a good time."

"Sandy, I'm sorry to have to let you know, but the city is canceling the Festival of Trees celebration."

Sandy gasped.

Chapter Twenty-Five

Natalie returned from her walk with three missed calls, two texts and one worried voicemail from Sandy. She redialed the number and immediately heard the urgency in Sandy's voice.

The Festival of Trees final celebration was canceled.

The city would not be providing funding or offering support from the police to block off the streets like they had done in the past.

Budget cuts, they said, but Natalie knew better. This had Eli Collins written all over it. All of his talk about not understanding the appeal of Christmas wasn't just talk.

* * *

Eli took a last bite of his sandwich before tossing the container in the trash. His phone rang at his desk.

"Eli Collins," he answered.

"You have a visitor," his secretary said. "May I send her in?"

"Sure." Hannah had texted him earlier that morning that she would drop by to pick up Luke's soccer cleats that he had left in Eli's car the night before.

He went back to answering an email and just as he was about to hit send he heard a strong knock on the door and the sound of his office door opening. He turned around in his chair and wanted to sink into the floor.

Natalie.

"What are you doing here?" Eli asked.

"The receptionist let me in."

"She shouldn't have done that," he mumbled.

"You thought I wouldn't come after you canceled the Live Nativity and finale celebration?"

"Well you didn't respond to any of my texts, so no, I didn't think you'd come talk to me."

Natalie crossed her arms. Eli began to explain. "It's nothing personal about your little Live Nativity. The city's budget is hemorrhaging, and the board had to make some tough decisions. It's not personal, I promise you that." *I tried to save it,* he wanted to add. *I wanted to save us.*

"Nothing is ever personal with you, is it?" Natalie shook her head.

Eli shifted through some folders on his desk. He found the one he was looking for and attempted to hand it to Natalie.

"It isn't cost-effective to devote so much of Harbor Ridge's resources to one evening that isn't going to bring in any revenue. It makes no sense on paper. Look at the numbers from the last few years. The hospital can still have their auction and donations through an online format, but the city can't fund the celebration event."

Natalie shook her head.

"You knew how hard I was working on this event. If you knew the city wasn't going to fund it, why did you lead me on?"

Eli dropped the folder back on his desk in disgust. His head immediately went to the fight that ended his relationship with Kendra. He had gotten two job offers and wanted to take the one in another state and thought she'd be fine to move with him. That's what they had agreed on. Now, here he was again being accused of the same thing. There was nothing he valued more than his honesty and integrity, even if it came across as harsh sometimes. He took a deep breath to settle himself.

"I did not lead you on. It's not like I was the only one on the decision. The board has already made up their mind. There isn't anything I can do," he said.

"Fine. You can be the one to tell Quinn about it. That her uncle doesn't care about whether she has a good Christmas or not," she added.

Eli stood up from his desk and rushed after her. "You are out of line. Don't make this about Quinn or Luke."

He looked down at her eyes and noticed for the first time, the sparkle in her eyes that he had started falling in love with was no longer there. He wanted to crawl under his desk.

"Can I make it about me?"

Her voice cracked as she brushed a tear off her cheek. "You knew how important this event was to me. How much it meant to me." She took a deep breath. "And none of that mattered to you. You don't care. You've made it clear how you feel about Christmas. So you coming to the Christmas pageant? The diner afterwards? The Chamber dinner? All of it meant nothing to you? I meant nothing to you."

Natalie left before he was able to get a word out to explain. If she meant nothing to him then why was she the only thing he kept thinking about since the Chamber dinner. For a few minutes he sat in silence.

This was exhausting.

Eli finished up responding to his last email before closing his laptop and sitting back in his chair. He needed to clear his head. He grabbed his gym bag from the closet and left the office.

He locked his car and walked toward the gym. He pulled out his keycard to let himself through the turnstile.

"Eli?"

He would recognize that voice anywhere.

Chapter Twenty-Six

He turned and was face to face with Amy. Could this day get any worse? Her features were the same as he remembered. She probably couldn't say the same about his receding hairline. Her hair was wet, pulled back in a high ponytail.

"I tried texting you. I may not have had the right number."

Eli fumbled through his words. Now with her standing right in front of him, he felt dumb for not responding to her. Four years was a long time, but looking at her felt like yesterday.

"What are you doing here?"

Amy spoke softly. "Swimming."

Eli looked down. "I mean what are you doing in Harbor Ridge?"

"What about you? I didn't know you lived here, either."

"Just temporarily."

Amy looked around, her ponytail making a wet spot on her green hoodie.

"You should dry your hair before you get out in the cold. You don't want to get sick."

She picked up her ponytail. "You sound like Dad." She looked him up and down. "And you're starting to look like him too."

Eli smiled. She did notice his hairline. "I'll take that as a compliment."

"Good, because I meant it as one. Can I have a hug?" Amy asked.

"Of course."

They embraced.

Amy looked down to the floor, "I wasn't sure you wanted to see me. Hannah doesn't."

"Honestly, I didn't know."

Amy sighed. "I'm just tired of running away."

Eli let out a deep breath. *Running away.* He could relate. Since their parents passed away, Eli had had six contract jobs in four different states. Maybe he and Amy weren't so different after all.

"How long have you been swimming?"

"Not too long. Matt, my um, fiancé, was a swimmer in high school. It's very relaxing."

She paused before looking up at him.

"What's going on with you?"

"Matt wanted us to come be with his mom for Christmas and he's been begging me to talk to you Hannah and you again. He doesn't want us getting married with his whole family there and me not have anyone."

"I see. Do you want us there?"

Amy nodded. "I do, very much so. All these milestones are coming up. Getting married and graduating college, hopefully if I can get it together. I wish I had people to share it with."

"Of course. That's what a family is supposed to be about. Sharing the good and the bad. That's what hurt so much when you left. We just wanted to be there for you."

"I know. I thought if I left, I wouldn't feel the pain anymore. It wouldn't hurt as much. But it did."

Eli felt that in his bones.

"Why did you come back?"

Amy looked around the room. "It's not only that of course. Matt thinks I'm holding myself back by not dealing with everything. Not having closure."

"You're saying what Matt thinks. What do you think?"

"I just miss everyone." She bit her lower lip as tears fell down her cheeks.

Eli blinked back tears. "We've missed you too."

"I thought you and Hannah hated me. Mom and Dad were on their way to pick me up when the accident happened. If I would have been at home it never would have happened."

"Amy, we never blamed you. Never. It was an accident. You're not to blame for any of that. Is that why you didn't want to see us?"

"I was scared and didn't know what to say. The longer I went without visiting or talking, the easier it was, I guess."

"You're doing okay now? Getting ready to graduate and get married?"

"Yep. One more year of school left. I really struggled freshman year and failed a few classes. I was about to drop out but my science professor, Dr. Haren, convinced me to try one more semester. She didn't give up on me. Had some tough love but never gave up on me. Now she's my advisor. I'm going to be a High School Science teacher like her. Maybe I can help kids like she did for me."

Amy's face lit up talking more about her chemistry class and experiments they got to do in their science lab. "That's how Matt and I met. We were lab partners sophomore year."

"And now you want to be life partners?"

Amy smirked. "You're still coming through with the dad jokes."

Eli smiled as he shrugged his shoulders. "I'll take that as a compliment."

"You seemed in a hurry to leave. I hope I'm not keeping you."

Eli looked down at his watch. "Just hoping to get a workout in before the pool closes. Are you staying in Harbor Ridge through Christmas?"

"Yes, I'm staying at Matt's mom's house. That is, unless his mom kicks me out. We're not getting along very well. I guess I have that effect on people these days."

"The holidays are stressful. I'm sure it's not just you. " Eli remembered Amy being rather high maintenance as a teenager so it was possible the conflict was two sided as most conflicts typically are.

"I haven't been able to talk to Hannah yet. I want to but she doesn't want to talk to me."

"I know the feeling." Amy looked at him with a confused look on her face. He scratched the side of his forehead. "It's a long story, don't ask."

"Oh right, is this about Natalie?"

Wow, this really is a small world. "How do you know Natalie?"

"Matt's mom is working with Natalie on the Festival of Trees project. Or I guess she *was* working on it. That was a pretty crummy thing to do, to go ahead and cancel it."

"I didn't cancel it. The town . . ." Eli let out a big sigh. He wanted to pry more from Amy about if she knew how Natalie was doing and how she felt about him but this wasn't the time or place.

"I want to get together again but if I don't get some of this energy out I'm going to go crazy. Can we meet again?"

"Of course. Do you want to get dinner sometime this week?" Eli nodded.

Eli gave her a hug goodbye. Well at least one of his relationships was on the mend. It was though he could feel the pain leaving his body. He smiled as he walked toward the locker room.

Chapter Twenty-Seven

"Linda told you?" Natalie looked up from her monitor, her eyes still red from her meeting with Eli during lunch and from staring at her computer scene all morning sending emails and undoing spreadsheet after spreadsheet. She squinted and nodded. Rachel sighed and shook her head. She walked around the cubicle and scooted her chair next to Natalie's.

"I'm sorry I wanted to be the one who told you. I didn't know things would happen so soon. I . . ."

Natalie tilted her head, "Well Sandy was the one who told me, because it affects the Live Nativity most of all."

Rachel's eyes looked around their office. "Oh." She looked down at the floor. She took a deep breath. "I have to tell you something. I got a new job. My last day here is next Friday."

Natalie felt like the bottom fell out of her stomach. She closed her eyes and sighed. *How could this be happening?*

"I can't believe you're leaving right now. I thought you wanted to stay at least three to five years? Wasn't that your plan?"

Rachel nodded. "I thought it was, but an opportunity came up at the bank and it was too good to pass up. I didn't think they would ever hire me, but they did and want me to start before the end of the year."

Sometimes Natalie wished she could channel half of Rachel's confidence into her own life.

For the second time that week, Natalie felt blindsided. Overwhelmed, she grabbed her jacket and walked outside to get some fresh air. The sky was a crisp blue, not a cloud in the sky. She sat down on her favorite bench that overlooked the entire courtyard. She couldn't help but smile at all of the trees. They were quite the sight and it wouldn't be long before the courtyard would go back to being empty. She noticed a group of friends taking selfies in front of one of the trees. As she watched them interact, she felt guilty for how she had treated Rachel. Rachel was her friend and she had been anything but a friend to her. She looked up and saw Rachel walking toward her.

"Can I join you?"

Natalie looked up and saw Rachel holding two cups of coffee. She smiled.

"I should be buying you coffee. I'm sorry I reacted poorly."

Rachel shook her head. "No, I'm sorry. I didn't know they'd want me to start so soon. Or that the Festival was going to be canceled. I thought I'd be leaving at the right time. Instead, it seems like a mess."

Natalie laughed. "The perfect time to leave."

"No, I don't want to leave things in a mess for my friend."

"Regardless, I should be happy for you. This sounds like a great opportunity."

"Thank you," she smiled. "I'm going to miss it here, especially this time of year. This is my favorite Christmas display in the city."

Natalie smiled. It was hers too.

They quickly made their way back to the office and the whole way back, Natalie thought about how she hoped they'd get someone good as a replacement.

Natalie could hear Rachel take off each post-it note from her monitor, wad it up and throw it in the trashcan on the other end of her cubicle.

After her last fluorescent colored yellow post-it note went into the trash, she turned to Natalie. "Well on the bright side, now I can work on the Valentine's Day event."

"That's one way to look at it, I suppose."

"I take it you're still sad the festival is not going to be happening this year?"

Natalie swiveled around in her computer car. She made eye contact with Rachel and nodded. She quickly turned back around to keep from getting too emotional about it.

"I understand. It feels like all we've done the last three weeks is work on it. You'd think they could have made their decision about this earlier. Could have saved us a lot of time."

Natalie nodded. Of course it would have, but that would've required Eli to think about anyone else besides himself. Which was apparently impossible for him to do. Except, of course, if it was for Quinn or Luke.

The new plan was for all the trees to remain on the hospital plaza until the beginning of the New Year. If the donors had added the ornaments to their gift baskets, the winning bidders would also receive the ornaments from the donated tree as well. In addition to contacting all the donors about the cancellation of the finale Night, Rachel and Natalie had the mundane tasks of uploading each of the tree and its contents to a newly created website. In essence doing the same job twice. Instead of picking up their items at the night of the Live Nativity and finale celebration, the items would be picked up the week the 22nd and 23rd. Natalie and some of the administrative team would now also be in charge of making sure the baskets and gifts arrived in time. And that they had a place to store them.

Natalie put in her ear buds to focus on entering the data to their spreadsheet. Rachel tapped on her shoulder and she jumped.

"It's going to be okay, I promise."

"When is your last day again?" Natalie asked with a smirk.

"Friday."

Natalie brought her hand to her forehead and pretended to faint.

Chapter Twenty-Eight

"Excuse me." Sandy pushed her shopping cart to the right of the aisle to make room for a young couple before attempting to grab an item off the top of the shelf. Sandy stood on her tiptoes and knocked a box of the premade muffin mix to the ground.

The young man walked over to her. "Ma'am could I help you get something?"

Everything in Sandy wanted to decline his offer. Asking for help had always been difficult for her. He must have been at least six foot five, even taller than Matt. He reached for the top shelf and easily grabbed a box of the muffin mix. She smiled at him as he went back to a young woman she assumed was his girlfriend.

The couple walked down the crowded aisle holding hands. Oh to be young and in love! Her mind immediately went back to Matt and Amy. What a mess they were in, and it was her fault. Matt had been standoffish since they arrived. At first she'd thought she wanted Matt and Amy to break up. She hadn't seen how they went together or had much in common. But she hadn't realized how much Matt was in love with Amy. She could see it in his eyes when Amy walked out the door. It was though his heartbeat had left his body.

A feeling came over Sandy in the middle of the frozen food section. The Holy Spirit comes in unexpected times and in unexpected ways. Suddenly Sandy felt moved to act. It wasn't enough to show up in the community or church with a smile on her face, serving others, if she couldn't serve her own family. If she couldn't love her own family. And whether she was ready or not, Amy was going to be her family.

God, please let me learn to love Amy like Matt loves her. No, let me learn to love her, like You love her.

Sandy continued to the frozen food section and saw the same couple she had previously seen picking out a box of vegan butter. Sandy was taken back by the price tag but she knew she had to start somewhere.

"Hi," Sandy smiled. The young woman smiled back. "Hi."

Sandy rubbed her hands together before asking nervously, "I'm sorry to bother you. My daughter-in-law—well, future daughter-in-law—is visiting and she's vegan and I'm in over my head with what to cook and make. What do you recommend to cook for dinner? I've been Googling recipes and I don't know where to start. I don't mean to intrude, but I happened to notice your cart items and thought you could help me."

The couple smiled at each other. "Of course. That is awesome you're stocking your kitchen for her. We're here buying our own food because my family thinks we're crazy. She's lucky to have you."

Sandy bit her lip. No one was lucky with how she had been acting the last few days. Selfishly holding onto how things used to be. Putting her perfect meal ahead of her relationship with her son. She hoped Matt and Amy could work out their differences. She wouldn't stand in the way anymore.

After spending more on groceries than she had since Matt was a teenager and playing lacrosse, Sandy pulled into the garage. She popped the trunk. She heard footsteps and turned to be face-to-face with Matt. The exhaustion and heartache present in his tired eyes. He grabbed a few grocery bags and turned back to the house. Even being upset with her, he still wanted to help. He was a good kid. A good young man. When did that happen? She didn't want to glamorize how challenging being a single parent was or that every moment wasn't all sunshine and rainbows, but in that moment all she thought of was: *Did I make it count enough, God? Did I worry enough about what really mattered?*

"Matt?" Sandy spoke softly. He turned and shrugged his shoulders. Some days she still couldn't believe that her little boy was taller than her.

"Yes, Mother."

Mother. A slight dig. She could feel the frustration in his voice.

Matt continued, "Amy's having dinner with her brother tonight. She may end up staying there the rest of the time. Can't say I blame her."

He continued walking back to their kitchen.

"Matt. I'm so sorry." Sandy spoke softly.

"Yeah, me too."

Sandy opened the refrigerator and made room for her new ingredients.

"What's all this?" Matt asked, confused as he held up a box of vegan butter.

"I thought we could make Christmas cookies tomorrow if Amy wants to join us."

"Is this a peace offering?"

Sandy gave Matt a hug.

"Yes. Can we start over?"

"I'll text Amy and see if she wants to come over. But Mom, we have to talk. Amy and I want to get married and I want you to be okay with it, but ultimately I have to do what's best for me. Please don't put me in a position where I have to choose."

Sandy took a deep breath.

"I just want you to be happy." She paused, knowing she shouldn't add conditions but couldn't help herself. "But I really want you both to finish college first. There are so many other pressures that come with being married and figuring life out. I know you think I'm old fashioned, but trust me on this."

"Of course Mom. That was always the plan."

Sandy was confused. "Amy said she had another year left or so."

"She does and we don't plan on getting married until next summer."

"Not *this* summer?"

Matt shook his head. "No Mom, we were never getting married this summer."

Sandy laughed to herself. All of that worry for nothing. Matt shook his head.

"I tried to talk to you about it, but you kept shutting me down. We've always been able to talk about anything."

Sandy nodded. He was right. They had always shared a close bond. For most of his life, it had been the two of them. As hard as it was for Sandy to admit, knowing it was no longer going to be the two of them stung. Change, even expected change, was hard. What if she switched her mindset to being happy for a new addition to the family, instead of losing Matt? Could there be beauty to come in the future?

* * *

Eli sat at a corner table sipping on his Coke and waiting for Amy to arrive. He needed the caffeine after a long day at work. Amy was usually at least fifteen minutes late, sometimes more. When they were younger it was a running family joke. Who was going to show up first, Hannah or Amy? Tonight was no different. Twenty-one minutes later, Amy appeared through the front door of the restaurant.

"Sorry I'm late," Amy said as she slid into the booth.

"Thanks for meeting me tonight. I hate that Matt couldn't join us. I hope to meet him some time."

Amy shrugged as she took a sip of water.

"Everything going okay with you two?"

Amy set her glass on the table and exhaled. "I walked in on Matt telling his mom he didn't want to get married. He's sorry but it still hurts."

Eli tried unsuccessfully to hide his shock. They had literally just gotten engaged as far as he knew. Amy was so young.

"I think he wanted to tell his mom what she wanted to hear. She doesn't like me very much. He's having dinner with her tonight. I think it'll be good for them to spend some time together without me there. That way we're not all tiptoeing around the house."

"Why doesn't she like you very much? She doesn't know you very well."
I don't know you very well any more, either. A lot can change in four years.

Amy twirled her hair around her index finger. "I'm just not what his mom expected. I think she wishes I wasn't around so she could spend more time with Matt alone. It's just been the two of them for a long time. Christmas has always been just the two of them."

"What does Matt think of all of it?"

Amy stirred her drink. "He feels bad. We'll talk more tonight when I get back. I'm sure he's trying to help his mom find a new location for the Live Nativity. I think she is close to giving up though. There's just not enough time."

Eli shook his head. "No, they're not able to have it. The city couldn't budget for it and unfortunately had to cancel it."

"Matt's mom thought they might move it to their church or something like that. Her and Natalie didn't want all the rehearsals to go to waste."

Eli got it now. Somewhere on private property. Somewhere where they wouldn't have to use city funding. He wondered if Natalie had anything to do with that.

"Natalie's pretty bummed. Since her wedding was canceled, she finally had something else fun to look forward to in December. I mean besides Christmas obviously."

"Her wedding? What are you talking about? When was this?"

"A few years ago. She was engaged and the guy broke it off right after they sent out their wedding invitations."

"That's awful." He would relate to how she must have felt.

"She told me she had always dreamed of having a beautiful Christmas wedding. Christmas events are her favorite."

"She told me she had been engaged before, but she never told me she was going to get married in December."

Eli ran his fingers through his hair. That's why this event was so important to her. It was a chance for her to have a meaningful Christmas. A chance to replace bad memories with good ones. A chance to reclaim Christmas.

"I know Matt's mom has been involved with this festival for ages since it started. It means a lot to her too. Something she can control." Amy laughed.

Eli tapped his fist on the table. He thought back to that first night he saw Natalie, wearing that tacky silver Santa sweater, ringing the bell outside the grocery store, the way her eyes sparkled.

"We have to figure out a way to save it."

Amy squinted at him. "How are we supposed to do that? I don't know anything about how to host a festival."

"Everything was handled, right? It's just the location we need to find?"

"I suppose. I can talk to Matt's mom and see what's going on. How's Hannah doing?" Amy looked at him as if to plead for him to help her. He wasn't sure how to answer that question. He didn't know how, but he was determined to put his family back together. Suddenly he got an idea.

"What are you going to do tomorrow?"

Amy shrugged. "Nothing that I know of."

Eli had an idea, but he didn't know if it was going to happen. As he drove home, he prayed for the first time he could remember in a long time. He wanted to put his family back together and he knew it would take a strength greater than he had for it to happen.

* * *

Hannah took one last sip of coffee before setting it back in her console. She was a few minutes late to meeting Eli to work out together. Getting the kids to school had been a challenge. Ben had been called away to a meeting and she forgot to make their lunches the night before like she usually did. Not a great way to get the day started.

Hannah put her hand on the door to the gym before letting go as she heard her name being called. She turned to see Eli sitting on the bench outside the gym.

She smiled. "Hey." His face turned to the parking lot. Hannah's eyes looked toward the lot to see what he was looking at. She felt her heart beating faster and her stomach twist.

Hannah turned back to Eli abruptly. "What is she doing here?"

Eli stood up from the bench and put his hands on Hannah's shoulder. "I gave her a chance. You should too. Can't we all just move on together? And leave the past in the past?"

Hannah felt like she'd been punched in the stomach. Now Eli was taking sides. Didn't anyone care about her? What she'd been through?

Hannah looked up at the building to avoid making eye contact with either one of them.

"Hannah?" Amy spoke softly as if she was bracing for anything.

Hannah continued gazing away from her, not wanting to acknowledge her presence.

Amy walked around her. "Come on Eli, let's go. This is a waste of time."

Eli sighed heavily motioning toward Hannah. "You've always been the one I've looked up to. The one who's been level-headed about all kinds of things. I guess I expected too much from you this time."

His comment cut deep. There was no way he was going to blame this all on her. Amy was gone for years, but he wasn't going to let her take a few weeks to gather herself? No way was she going to let him off the hook for that comment.

"I'm so glad the two of you can be the perfect picture of harmonious siblings, and it sure was nice of you both to leave me with the mess of trying to figure out everything after Mom and Dad died."

She turned toward Amy, feeling in her gut, *Don't say it, don't say it.* "I'm sure you enjoyed the inheritance you got, though."

"Hannah!" Eli looked horrified. Amy hung her head.

"My children don't even know who you are." Amy looked up at her. Her hazel eyes filled with tears. Hannah stared back in anger. But as their eyes met, Hannah was filled with regret.

"At least Mom and Dad got to hold your babies," Amy said. "See you get married. Walk you down the aisle. You have memories I'll never get to have."

Hannah gritted her teeth. "Memories? You mean the pictures I can't look at anymore? Having to tell my kids we can't go to grandma and grandpa's house? Listening to my five-year-old cry herself to sleep? But I had it so easy?"

"You had Ben and your kids. I had no one."

Hannah looked at Eli, who looked like he was regretting ever thinking this meeting was a good idea.

"You would have had a family, but you abandoned us. And by family, do you mean my husband who travels more for work during the month than he is home. The husband I was separated from for six months before we got back together last year. " Hannah looked at Eli and her aggravation grew with his silence.

Amy looked shocked. "I didn't know."

"Yeah, you didn't know. Because you weren't here. And I don't know why you decided to come back here now." Before Amy could respond, she added, "And honestly, I don't care."

Amy, with her head down, passed her and walked into the gym. Hannah glanced up at Eli who had a look on his face she'd never seen before. Disappointment. He shook his head. There was nothing for him to say.

Eli walked past her. Hannah sat down on the bench and put her head in her hands. It was supposed to feel different. She was supposed to feel better. All those years she had spent rehearsing exactly what she wanted to say to Amy if she got the chance. Exactly how she was going to make Amy feel just as bad as she had been made to feel.

Hannah didn't know it was going to make her feel that much worse. Looking into Amy's eyes felt like staring into a mirror. Looking at a reflection of sadness, of exhaustion, of grief.

Chapter Twenty-Nine

Natalie sat in her apartment deciding between vacuuming or laundry. What a thrill. Usually on the weekends in December she'd be off shopping at a holiday craft fair, ice skating, or reading some cheesy feel-go predictable romance. She wasn't in the mood for any of those things these days. It was hard to get herself in her usually jolly mood when all she wanted to do was rewind the last six weeks and start over.

Natalie paced around her kitchen thinking about where to go from here. All her hard work the last year on the festival and especially the past few months had been for nothing. What hurt the worst was Eli knowing what she was working on. He knew and he did nothing to even let her or Sandy know that it was a possibility the festival might be canceled. How many hours upon hours had been a waste?

Her phone dinged, rescuing her from reliving the past. She had done a ton of work to not live in the past and to move forward, but lately it seemed like those old habits were coming back.

It was a note from Sandy. *We're making cookies if you want to stop by.* Natalie hesitated, but the more she thought about it the more she welcomed the distraction from Eli and the now-canceled festival.

Natalie walked into Sandy's house and was immediately greeted by the smell of warm sugar and cinnamon and the soft sound of Christmas music playing on the bluetooth speaker in the kitchen. Natalie joined Sandy, Matt, and Amy baking cookies. They were going to take them for some of the senior adults from the church.

Sandy stood overseeing Amy and Matt as they worked together completing the cookie recipes, grabbing the right utensils and mixing bowls so they could keep each recipe separate.

The best way to lift your mood is to help someone else, Sandy liked to say, and she was right. Pretty soon, Natalie forgot all about her fight with Eli and their Live Nativity that was barely hanging on.

Amy worked carefully making vegan chocolate chip cookies. She kept separate bowls and utensils to avoid cross-contamination.

"We could make twenty dozen cookies for the amount of money it cost to make one dozen of your vegan cookies," Sandy whispered to Matt.

"Mom!" Matt scolded. "You said you were going to try harder. Please."

"Okay, okay." Sandy made eye contact with Natalie. She nodded.

Amy asked, "Have you been able to find another location for the Live Nativity?"

"It's *always* been outside the church, but it doesn't look like that is going to be able to happen this week." Sandy said.

"Well just because it's *always* been one way doesn't mean it can't change," Amy said.

"Yeah, somewhere new could bring in a bigger audience?" Matt added as he gave Amy a side hug.

Natalie thought for a second. The church gym? The sanctuary? The sets they had used were designed specifically for outside and there was no way they could have live animals in the building.

"What we need is a farm. A big farm."

Amy opened the fridge to put back the butter and noticed a glass bottle of milk on the shelf with a circle label. She looked down at it as a flood of memories came back. "Patterson Farms. I know the people who run it. I mean, assuming it's the same people from five years ago? Mr. Patterson was my dad's college roommate. They were more like brothers."

Natalie took a deep breath. This was the first time Amy had ever said anything about her parents.

Sandy shook her head. "They book months or even years in advance for weddings. I have no doubt they will be reserved on the 22nd, especially since it's a Saturday."

Amy set the bottle back down and hung her head.

Natalie gave her a hug and whispered. "Thanks for trying. I've had to accept that it's just not going to happen this year. Sometimes we have to move on."

Amy sighed as she stirred in the dairy-free chocolate chips.

Two hours later, the countertops were covered in nearly a hundred cookies. They packaged up the cookies and all four of them set off in Sandy's minivan. Natalie sat in the passenger seat helping navigate to each address.

Their first stop was for an older man and woman who were home-bound. They were members of the church. Matt volunteered to go with Sandy to deliver the cookies at the first house.

Natalie took off her seat belt and turned to the backseat where Amy sat.

"This afternoon has been fun. I really needed the distraction. I had no idea vegan chocolate chip cookies could be so delicious."

Amy put her phone down that she had been scrolling. "I honestly don't miss the other kind at all."

"It was nice of Sandy to get all of the ingredients."

"It was. Was it just me, or did it still feel tense?"

Natalie wouldn't deny the obvious. "I think it had less to do with you and more with the frustration we feel about the festival being canceled."

"I'm sorry about my brother. He can be really stubborn."

"Sounds about right." Natalie had to stop herself from going down the rabbit hole of her terrible conversations with Eli.

"Have you heard from Hannah at all?" Natalie asked.

"I don't want to talk about it. I thought if I came back, if I tried, things would be okay. It feels like she's never going to forgive me, and I can't blame her."

"You're here now and trying. Sometimes it's not up to us, but don't give up. Maybe she just needs some space." Natalie answered.

"I wish things were different," Amy said.

"Me too."

Chapter Thirty

Eli took a deep breath before he made the familiar walk up the five brick stairs to Hannah's house. An ornate green wreath with red and white ribbons hung on the door. He remembered a similar wreath their mother would put up every year. He paused for a moment as the vision of Christmas when he was growing up played in his head.

He could see his parents' living room, fully decorated. It was a rush to get down the stairs and open presents. Each of their monogrammed stockings in front of three wrapped gifts. He was always the one patiently waiting at the top of the stairs. Their mom eagerly waiting with him in her comfy blue robe. Their dad with the large video camera on his shoulder, taping every moment. Those were the memories of his childhood. Usually Hannah and Amy would trade gifts or most likely Amy would grab something of Hannah's and run around the house. His mom would go after Amy and Eli would run after Hannah trying to keep the baby doll or sweater intact.

He was stuck in the middle of his sisters again. If only their mom was here to help fix this too. She could fix everything. Growing up he was frequently caught in between the girls, usually called to the family meeting as a witness. Life was much simpler when the stakes were a stretched-out sweater or borrowed butterfly clips. He loved them both so much and desperately wanted the three of them back together. He didn't know what it would take.

He rang the doorbell with his free hand and didn't have to wait long.

Hannah opened the front door, wearing her dark blue scrubs, her hair pulled back in a high ponytail, her eyeliner worn out around her eyes. She leaned up against the door frame and tilted her head to the side. She seemed both annoyed and relieved to see him.

Eli held out a plastic bag of takeout food in front of him. He knew she wasn't going to turn down a free dinner.

"Ben called me before he left on his trip this morning. He's worried about you." Hannah stood up from the door and turned around to walk into the house. He shut the door as Hannah took the bag of food from him. Eli followed her into the kitchen being careful to dodge the toys and backpacks that were strewed along the floor.

Hannah shook her head. "I wish he wouldn't have. The kids and I are fine." Hannah set the food on the kitchen counter after pushing some old magazines and newspapers out of the way.

"You look stressed."

Hannah quipped back, "Thanks."

Eli reached out to put his hand on her shoulder. Hannah swatted him away.

She put a hand on her hip while gesturing with her other arm. "Eli, I work full-time, have two kids and a husband who travels fifteen days out of every month. Who wouldn't be stressed?"

"And you haven't spoken to your sister in four years and now she's back wanting a relationship and you blew up at her. Does that cover it?"

Hannah bit her bottom lip. "I don't care that Amy's back. I don't care what Amy's doing. As far as I'm concerned, I don't have a sister anymore." She went back to untying the white plastic bag. When she couldn't get it untied, she hastily grabbed a pair of scissors and cut the bag.

Eli was not convinced. "You aren't any better at hiding your emotions than you were when we were kids. You obviously do care. And what is with this nonsense of *I don't have a sister anymore?* You had one for seventeen years before things got off track. You're willing to throw all of that away?"

Hannah scoffed.

"Remember when I borrowed Dad's car and backed into the garage?" Eli asked.

Hannah rolled her eyes. "If by *borrowed* you mean took without permission . . ."

"Yes."

Hannah folded her arms in front of her chest. "He was so mad at you. Him and Mom both. You were grounded forever. I had to chauffeur you around. It felt like my punishment, too."

"Seemed like it. But even that first night when they sent me to my room, they came and talked to me. I knew as mad as they were at me, they still loved me."

Eli moved closer to Hannah and put his hands on her shoulders. "Just like as mad as we are at Amy, we still love her. Mom would be heartbroken. You know she would be. How would you feel if Luke and Quinn decided to never speak again?"

Hannah wiped away a tear dripping down her face. Her demeanor changed and she pointed her finger at him.

"This isn't about Luke and Quinn, this is about me and Amy."

"They're watching you as you handle this, though. You can show them what it means to work through challenges. What it means to set an example."

Hannah shook her head. "I have every right to be angry at her. She abandoned our family. She left and decided she didn't want to talk to me anymore. But now that *she's* ready, I'm just supposed to forget everything she *didn't* do the last four years . . ."

"You're just supposed to *forgive*. Until you do that Hannah, the only person you're truly hurting is you. Haven't we all been hurt long enough?"

Hannah wiped another tear that leaked down her face and took a deep breath. Eli wasn't sure he could get through to her, but he wanted to try one last time.

"You remember senior year and the state semifinal track meet?"

Hannah cringed at the memory. "How could I forget? It's one of the most humiliating days of my life."

"Your relay team was in second place and you were about to pass the baton to Emerson and she dropped it."

"We were disqualified. All that work was for nothing. Why are you bringing this up?"

"Now hear me out. We talked about how passing the best things from Mom and Dad on was how we could honor and celebrate them. Mom and Dad gave us the gift of forgiveness and grace every day and we're not using it . . . we're dropping the baton."

Hannah looked up at him, her bloodshot eyes focused on him.

"And you?"

Eli took a breath not knowing how his next sentence would be met, "I've forgiven Amy for leaving and not keeping in touch. I know she's made her fair share of mistakes. We all have. I can't be angry at her anymore."

Hannah looked at him with a glare of betrayal. "I thought we were a team on this."

Eli shook his head. "I wanted to know what she had to say. I thought she deserved the chance to explain herself. You're holding onto your anger and it's spilling into every avenue of your life. Your husband, your kids. Probably at your job. Whose head *haven't* you bit off this week? That's probably a shorter list."

Hannah threw down the dish rag she had been using to dry the pots and pans overwhelming her kitchen counters. "Maybe you and Amy are close again because you're both selfish."

"Selfish?" Eli could feel his heart beating faster. Was he about to be on the receiving end of Hannah's rage?

She nodded. "Yeah, I told you not to date Natalie and you did it anyway. With zero consideration how losing my friend would feel. Not to mention that the kids are asking about her and I don't have a good answer."

"Well, take it up with her. That's the problem with girls, you all just talk around each other, instead of with each other."

Hannah's eyes shot right through him.

"Women."

"Thank you, I guess. You haven't stayed anywhere long enough to make an effort with anyone. Certainly not with Natalie. Whatever was going on with her, you're flaky."

Her words stung as they came at him. His first thought was to deny it. He wanted to yell back at her and point out more of her shortcomings. That would have been easier. To walk out and slam the door and push down his feelings like he was used to. He was tired of the fighting. He realized she was right. He knew he had made a mistake and he wanted to change.

"That's fair for you to say. I haven't done the best opening myself up to relationships. I thought if I kept to myself I could avoid feeling anything at all, but that's not how life works."

Hannah crossed her arms in front of her chest. Exasperated, she asked, "What do you want from me, Eli?"

He took a few steps toward her and put his hand on her shoulder. This time she let him.

"I wish you could give Amy a chance to talk to you about what life has looked like the last four years. I know she hasn't done everything right."

"*Anything* right. Anything at all."

"Maybe you'll realize that you both have more in common than you think. I know we did."

Hannah backed up from him and shook her head. "I'm sorry, but I'm not ready to do that."

It was what he expected, but it still hurt him to hear her say those words.

With a look of despair and defeat Hannah continued, "And I don't know that I ever will be."

Eli nodded and turned to walk out the door. Maybe it was time for him to move on from ever thinking things could change. To ever thinking his family could get put back together. He was tired of the chaos.

But he wasn't ready to give up yet.

Chapter Thirty-One

Natalie sprinted from her car and hurriedly pulled the door to the gym open. The warm air inside was a welcome relief from the chill. She'd accidentally set her alarm for p.m. and had nearly overslept. Stephanie was out sick this week and Natalie welcomed the distraction of subbing for her aerobics class. She knew she would be sitting at her office chair for the rest of the day.

As she rushed up the stairs, she noticed an attractive guy lifting shirt up to wipe the sweat off his face. As his shirt came down, Natalie's stomach fell.

Eli.

Their eyes quickly connected and as Eli's mouth opened, Natalie hung her head and darted past him. He quickly stepped diagonally in front of her with his long gait.

"Hey, are you ever going to stop giving me the silent treatment?"

Natalie lifted her head, her eyes looking down. She did not want to have this conversation. "I have to go to class."

Eli looked at the clock behind her head. "It's 8:41. You have four minutes."

Natalie moved her eyes up connecting with Eli's for the first time since she left his office. "I think you said enough at the party and at your office. Anything else you want to add?"

She looked in his eyes wanting any sign of an apology or admission and it just wasn't there.

"Just tell me this. *When* did you know the city wouldn't fund the festival?"

Eli raised his eyebrow, "Huh?"

Natalie wasn't playing games. She spoke slowly on purpose, her voice slightly raised, "When did you know?"

Eli's long gaze shifted to the floor. "Some discussion started happening at the breakfast meeting a few weeks ago."

Natalie's stomach sunk even further than when she first saw him that morning. Her chest tightened as she whispered, "That's all I needed to know."

She didn't turn back as she heard him call her name.

Natalie quickly walked down the hallway into the group exercise room. She dropped her bag in the corner and picked up her wireless mic from the table. As she slowly threaded the mic through her tank top to fit in her pocket, she thought about Eli. How could he do that to her? Lead her on to think the festival was happening, when all along he'd known it wasn't? She'd been foolish to trust again. She quickly shut down those thoughts and focused on her playlist.

Her phone connected to the speakers and it was time to begin.

"Is this anyone's first time doing step?" She slowly turned around to the room full of participants.

* * *

Eli stood nervously in the back of the crowded room. How hard could this be? In forty-five minutes it would be over and he could hopefully continue talking to Natalie. She couldn't avoid him forever. Hannah talked about step class all the time and would have been in the class had it not been for an early shift. At least Hannah wouldn't be there to watch his humiliation.

He raised his hand to Natalie's question. Though he had frequently viewed the eye candy from the weight room during the forty-five-minute class, this was his first and probably last attempt at step aerobics. Natalie scrunched her eyebrow in annoyance at his attendance before turning her back to the class. She walked over to her phone that was plugged into the speaker and the music started.

Right basic step. Easy enough it was just up and down like walking up and down a set of stairs. Lunges? Easy peasy. He got this.

The first song ended and Natalie took a quick sip of water. "Okay guys, I'm going to show you a quick figure eight move and then we'll put it to the music. Ready? And five, six, seven, eight . . ."

Eli watched in awe as Natalie contorted her legs and quickly went from one side of the step to another. The participants in the class did the same.

Soon he determined he was not cut out for the concentration it took to not fall off the riser. He paused to take a water break. If Natalie noticed that he stopped she didn't let on.

He couldn't help but be drawn to her at that moment. Like they were the only two in the room. The way her ponytail bounced, her purple tank top sat tastefully just below her collarbone. Her smile is what most attracted him. She looked so happy in her element. The song finished and she walked over to the corner table to pick up her water bottle.

Her eyes quickly scanned the room. As their eyes connected, the smile she had the whole time she was leading faded. Eli felt his chest tightened. It was though her light had dimmed and she was no longer as bubbly.

"Everybody doing okay?" Natalie said in between sips of water. The room nodded in agreement. Natalie clapped her hands. "Let's put it all together."

"Great," Eli mumbled. He barely made it to the end of the class and had never felt more relief than when the cheesy slow country song came over the speaker and Natalie announced it was time for their cool-down.

The class ended and the participants slowly trickled out of the room. Eli stayed behind as he continued stretching his sore muscles. He didn't want his efforts to go unnoticed either. Natalie couldn't avoid him forever. His attempt was met with humor as Natalie walked over to him.

"You survived," she said, with a smile of amused disbelief.

No one was more shocked than he was that he'd stayed the entire forty-five minute class. "Barely." He continued stretching. "I'm going to feel this tomorrow."

Natalie shook her head. "What was it you called step aerobics before? A wimpy workout?"

Eli closed his eyes and sighed. Natalie giggled, scrunching up her nose and tilting her head back.

"Not bad for an old guy. You almost kept up with Mrs. Sloane."

Eli shook his head. "The woman next to me? She's like sixty years old."

"She's seventy-three."

Eli opened his mouth in shock. "What? No way."

"Yeah, isn't she incredible? I hope I'm in here having fun and in great shape when I'm her age."

Eli thought of Natalie in her seventies and thought she'd still be beautiful.

The room got emptier as people put their equipment away. Only he and Natalie were left. Natalie stuck out her hand to take part of the risers back.

Eli smiled at her. "Thanks."

Her face returned to its serious state, "No problem."

Natalie bumped into Eli as she put the risers away.

"Sorry," she said.

Eli stacked the risers on top of the pile and turned back to her. "Me too. I'm sorry, that is."

Her eyes changed right in front of him as if his apology was all she had been waiting for. He longed to embrace her and finally kiss her. That was the way he wanted their date at the Chamber dinner to end. Not with her not speaking to him.

"Natalie, I didn't know they were going to cancel the festival. I argued to keep it in the budget after our initial meetings about it. You have to believe me."

He needed her to believe him. He knew it was the truth, but how could he convince her?

"Why should I believe you? This is what you do."

"What is what I do?" Eli folded his arms in front of his chest, mirroring Natalie's stance.

She quickly uncrossed her arms. "You bounce around city to city completely detached from anything or *anyone* and call it economics without any consideration of how it affects people." She sounded as if she had been sitting on this thought for a while. "Whatever looks good on paper. Doesn't matter who gets hurt."

He stepped closer to her. "I was doing my job. I never meant to hurt you."

She backed up from him and crossed her arms again. "But you did."

And I've regretted it ever since, he thought. "Look, you were right at first. I did think the Festival of Trees was a waste, but you showed me it wasn't. I tried to convince the board. Tried to give them an alternative to all the spending cuts, but it was too late." He moved closer to her, but she backed away.

"It *is* too late."

It was now or never.

As he moved closer she stepped in until they were almost nose to nose. He wrapped his arm around her back, feeling the sweat that had soaked through. He pulled her closer and pushed his lips onto hers.

Her arms circled around his shoulders as she kissed him back. She ran her fingers over the outline of his biceps.

She caught her breath. A grin slowly emerged on her face.

"I've been wanting to do that for a long time." Eli smiled at her.

She smiled back at him before she scrunched her nose. "I smell."

He raised his eyebrow and smirked. "Only a little."

She pretended to elbow him. The smile he first fell in love making an appearance on her face again.

Finally.

She looked up at him.

Their kiss was everything he expected and then some. He wondered if they would ever get the chance to do it again.

He pulled her back into an embrace and she rested her head on his shoulder. The door to the gym room opened, the next instructor entered with a group of ladies ready for the next class.

Natalie suddenly pulled back from Eli's embrace. Eli reluctantly let go. Natalie's demeanor changed as if she had snapped back to reality.

"I've got to get to work."

"Me too."

* * *

Natalie unclenched her fists to grip her steering wheel. She needed to head to work but needed a few minutes to clear her head before she started her drive.

She had wanted Eli to kiss her since the night she saw him in the audience of the Christmas pageant. No one had ever looked at her like that before.

She visualized him sweeping her off her feet at the Chamber dinner. A kiss when he brought her home. Maybe sharing a kiss in the middle of the dance floor. What could have been more romantic? They didn't make it that far into the evening.

Instead their first and last kiss was in the smelly gym equipment room. On a day she was wearing no makeup and hadn't even showered before coming to class. Just like Eli to do something to catch her off guard.

Like canceling the Festival of Trees celebration.

None of it even mattered at this point anyway. He'd lied to her. Led her on. Knowing this entire time his job was to cut the city's budget and then move on to the next city where he would do the same thing.

What was his point of even coming to step class with her. Was she just a consolation kiss?

Natalie sat at her desk at work watching her coworkers leave nonchalantly to go to lunch. She had brought her lunch to work with her so she could continue working through the hour long break. There was an endless amount of paperwork to ensure that all of the donated silent auction prizes were uploaded online for the auction since they would no longer be able to hold it in person. *Thanks Eli.*

Natalie couldn't stay focused on finishing the spreadsheet about the auction for the Festival of Trees. Natalie angrily pounded on her keyboard. Her spreadsheet in Excel froze just as she was minutes away from updating their list.

"Do you want to take a break?" Rachel's unusually soft voice interrupting her concentration.

Natalie slowly turned in her seat and let out a long sigh.

"I would love a break." Natalie stood up and grabbed her coat. "Can we go for a quick walk? For the last time?"

Rachel hung her head. "Don't say it like that. I'll just be down the street after the first of the year. We can still meet for lunch."

Natalie nodded. It wouldn't be the same.

They walked along the sidewalk around the perimeter of the hospital, Natalie's boots crunching the salt the maintenance workers had placed in preparation for snow forecasted for later that afternoon. Natalie finally told Rachel about Eli showing up unannounced to her class.

Rachel's eyes doubled in size. "Did you like it?"

"No," Natalie said emphatically.

"Well then," Rachel said before adding, "That answers that. If there's no chemistry, there's nowhere to go. I've certainly kissed enough of them to know that."

Natalie laughed.

Rachel turned to her. "But when you were talking, your smile told a different story. Just saying."

Rachel walked ahead a few steps. Natalie shook her head but she couldn't keep a straight face. "Okay, well maybe it wasn't the worst kiss I've ever had."

Rachel nodded. "Uh huh."

"Okay, okay, so the kiss was great. I wish I would have had some warning. Or he could have kissed me before class. Before I was all sweaty and gross."

"Well maybe he wanted to kiss you before then. Didn't you say you've been avoiding him? Not returning his texts or calls?"

Natalie stopped and turned to Rachel. "Who's side are you on anyway?"

Rachel laughed. "I'm always on the side of love."

Natalie rolled her eyes. "Well you better look elsewhere than here, that's for sure."

They made it back to the courtyard entrance. It was bustling with people walking around checking out the trees and drinking coffee from one of the food trucks parked nearby.

Rachel overlooked the courtyard. "I'm going to miss this place."

"Me too. It's always so empty come January."

"Just not the spreadsheets."

They laughed. Natalie sipped her coffee and they continued on their loop before making it back to the administration entrance trying hard to keep her smile at bay.

Chapter Thirty-Two

Eli started a fire in his fireplace. He sat down in his recliner and flipped on the television. While he scrolled trying to find the perfect show, a loud knock at his door interrupted his search. For a brief moment, he thought it might be Natalie. No, he hoped it would be Natalie. He stopped himself from texting her. Clearly there was no question where he stood on his feelings for her. It was up for her to decide.

He quickly went to the front door and opened it. It was just Amy. This Amy was grinning ear-to-ear. The brightest smile since Eli had reconnected with her.

"Hey, what's going on?" Eli couldn't help but smile after seeing her big smile. Maybe her and Hannah had finally made amends.

Just as Eli was about to ask Amy what she was doing there, she reached down and pulled out an empty glass bottle and handed it to him.

"Thanks for the recycling?" Eli scratched his eyebrow more confused than ever as he took it from her hands.

Amy pointed to the front of the bottle. "No, no, look at the label."

Eli twisted the bottle around. *Patterson Farms.*

It took a moment, but soon Eli was flooded with memories of going to the pumpkin patch as a kid and touring the dairy farm with his school group in middle school. Riding four wheelers in high school and getting into mischief with his friends. Taking prom pictures with his date and on-and-off again high school girlfriend Julia.

"You remember, don't you?" Amy asked expectantly.

Eli nodded as he handed back the bottle. Mr. Patterson was his dad's college roommate and became more like a brother to him over the years. The two men played golf together and their families vacationed together when all the kids were younger. Mr. Patterson had made a point to check in with Eli periodically from time to time after his parents' death. It was never to be pushy but simply to know he was there if he was ever needed. Eli appreciated his friendship and guidance more than he had let on. He had never been the best about keeping in touch.

"I think we could have the festival there. I was just looking at their website," Amy reached in her pocket and pulled out her phone. She showed him pictures.

"You think it would work to have it on the farm? Doesn't the event need to be indoors with seating?" Eli thought of how it would work to have several hundred people outside on a working farm with parking and the live animals. There was no way it could work and not within the week time limit they had.

"A few years back they built an indoor venue where they have weddings and other events throughout the year. Sandy thinks they're probably booked already, but I had this feeling. To try at least."

Eli looked at her. "You want to ask them if they will donate their venue for the festival?"

Amy paused and looked up from her phone. She squinted her eyes. "No, I want you to ask them. Eli, I can't. If they mention Mom or Dad, I'll become a blubbering mess. I can't."

Her eyes sparkled with hope. She was so excited to possibly help save the festival. He had as hard of a time saying no to Amy as he did to Quinn and Luke. He knew the idea was a long shot. Even if the Pattersons said yes, how could the logistics even work?

"I will go with you and do the talking, but if this works you'll have to be the one to talk it over with Natalie and Sandy."

Amy threw her arms around him. She pulled up her phone. "I googled his number. I think this might be it. Is it the same one you have? Let's call him."

* * *

Thirty minutes later, Eli and Amy were driving up a long gravel road. Memories flooded back as they passed the lake they used to swim in during the hottest days in Harbor Ridge, the smaller barn where Eli had his first kiss with Julia. They passed a pasture of cows roaming around.

"Eli, stop!" Eli pushed on the brakes. In the middle of the driveway stood a magnificent deer.

"Wow, it's beautiful," Amy said.

They pulled in front of the family's grand farmhouse. A white wraparound porch lined the perimeter and the shutters on the house had been freshly painted.

They walked up the wooden stairs to the front door. Eli lightly knocked. The door swung open, revealing a man with white hair.

"Thank you for agreeing to meet with us on short notice," Eli began to say.

"Eli and Amy Collins?" The man grinned. His shoulders, broad and his hands calloused. He shook Amy's hand first. "I'd know that smile from anywhere. It's just like your mother's."

A tiny tear leaked from the corner of Amy's eye as she let out a deep breath. She grabbed hold of Eli's hand.

"Thank you," she muttered.

"Now what brings you two for a visit? Are you in town for Christmas?"

"Well Hannah and her family still live here. I've been doing a contract job with the city for the last few months." Eli took a step in the house. "Well I was hoping you could help us. We have run into a problem with the Festival of Trees celebration."

"Jackie and I used to go every year." His eyes became more solemn. He glanced at their portrait hanging above the fireplace. "She passed away last year."

"I'm so sorry," Eli and Amy said at the same time. Eli hung his head. Mrs. Patterson was always around their kitchen when Eli would visit. There was never a time where her home wasn't open and when she wasn't present making memories with her kids.

"Thank you," Mr. Patterson nodded. He turned back to them. "I bet her and your mother are having a blast together in heaven. They're probably decorating Christmas trees and signed up for the angel choir already."

Eli and Amy laughed. Eli thought about the laughter that would spill out over the living room when both families got together to celebrate. No matter the time that passed, their meetings together were like they had always been connected. Tonight was no different.

"Jackie loved the Christmas festival. For her it's what made Christmas Christmas. What seems to be the problem?"

Eli took a deep breath. "The city needed to rescind the contract for the festival due to budgeting issues."

Mr. Patterson shook his head. "You can never trust those government officials. What a rotten thing to do."

"Exactly," Amy said as she elbowed Eli. He tried to keep from giving her a look. As if he didn't feel bad enough.

Eli sighed. "Unfortunately, I was a part of that decision as much as I tried to avoid it. I know this is a long shot and you probably have a wedding or another event already booked, but we thought we could possibly have it on the farm?"

He scratched his eyebrow and thought. "What are the dates again?"

"It's for one night only. December 22nd."

Mr. Patterson's eyes grew wide. "Next Saturday, you mean. The Saturday before Christmas?"

"You're already booked?" Amy asked, trying to shield her disappointment.

Mr. Patterson motioned for them to come to the kitchen.

The house looked just as Eli remembered it. The gray couch still in the same place he spent watching movies with Julia and her brothers. The recliner her mom used to fall asleep in when they would be staying up too late.

Eli continued, "The decorated trees will stay where they are at in the courtyard of the hospital. The donations for that have been moved online. The only part of this event would just be the Live Nativity and food trucks. Of course we bring in trash cans and will have volunteers making sure we leave your farm the way we found it."

"We'll leave it better than we found it," Amy chimed in.

"Are you both in charge of the festival?"

Eli shook his head, "Sandy Nelson and Harbor Ridge Community Church are in charge of this part of the festival."

"Sandy's still doing the Nativity after all these years?" He smiled. "We went to school together. Grade school through high school."

Mr. Patterson motioned for them to follow him into his office. He opened his desk drawer to find his glasses. He slipped them on. They waited for his computer to boot up.

Eli held his breath. *God, please work this out.*

Mr. Patterson looked up and smiled.

"You're not going to believe this. We were booked with a wedding on the 22nd but it was canceled this week. We are available."

Eli exhaled.

"Now I'm going to have to talk with our operations manager tomorrow, but if you're bringing in all of the staff and also a clean up crew to set up and tear down. I don't see why we can't have it here." He looked down at the family picture next to his computer. "Jackie would be so pleased."

Eli looked over at Amy who was nearly bouncing off the walls with excitement.

"Thank you, thank you!" Amy gave Mr. Patterson such a big hug that she almost knocked him down.

"You're welcome, sweetie. Anything for the Collins family. Your parents were so good to us. I miss them and our Jackie."

"We do too. I'm sorry Jackie passed away."

"Me too. But I know she's in a better place than here."

Eli nodded. "We don't want to take any more of your time tonight. I appreciate it."

"Have the staff give us a call tomorrow and we'll do our best to work everything out."

Amy gave Mr. Patterson another hug.

"Actually, can I have Sandy's number? I'll give her a call and see what we can work out together to get the ball rolling."

Amy pulled out her cell phone and scrolled to find Sandy's number. Mr. Patterson wrote the number down on a piece of paper.

Eli and Amy walked out to the car. Amy had his information to pass along to Sandy as well. Mr. Patterson said he looked forward to connecting.

Eli looked around the farmhouse as they walked down the driveway. "I wish I knew that Mrs. Patterson had passed away. I would have tried to come to her funeral," Eli said sadly. He should have reached out to Julia at least, but he had been so consumed with work the last few years and with himself if he was being honest. He had missed so many opportunities to be there for his family and his friends. He wanted more now. He needed more in his life.

Amy nodded in agreement. "She was so glamorous. I remember she always looked flawless and had the sweetest heart. I bet her and Mom *are* having fun up there."

He noticed Amy glance up at the clear dark blue sky with just a sprinkle of white stars. Eli looked at her and felt what she did. For the first time in years, there was an overwhelming peace in their lives. A peace that transcends all understanding.

Amy smiled even bigger than she had earlier in the day when she dropped by unannounced. "I can't believe we got him to say yes."

"You were great. Thank you for helping me with this."

"You think Natalie will be surprised?"

"Big time."

Eli looked down to the steering wheel. "Don't tell her I had anything to do with it."

"Why not? You'll be her hero." Amy asked, genuinely confused.

Eli could see it going in a different direction. "Because if she knows, then she won't come to it and I want her to be able to come and enjoy it."

Chapter Thirty-Three

Sandy read a magazine on the couch. Well, pretended to, anyway. Matt and Amy were making dinner in the kitchen and as much as she wanted to, no she needed to oversee, she had to tell herself to park it on the couch. They wanted a chance to cook for her and she needed to let them. She loved cooking but she could get used to this treatment. If only she could relax with someone else in her kitchen.

They were making barbecue tacos. Well she wasn't too sure about how they were going to pull off the barbecue "meat" part of it, but she didn't want to be too skeptical. She tried to sneak into the kitchen twice under the guise of helping with the dishes but was quickly shooed away.

"Mom, we've got this," Matt said assertively.

She nodded as her phone rang, taking her out of the kitchen.

She didn't recognize the number and almost didn't pick it up. Those scammers were making the rounds this time of year. Still something told her to answer.

"Hello, this is Sandra Nelson."

A familiar and stoic voice replied on the other end. "Hi Sandy, this is Jeffrey Patterson."

Sandy was not expecting to hear his voice on the other end. She turned away from the kitchen and smiled.

"Jeff, how are you?"

She hadn't seen him since his wife's funeral the previous year. She did not know his wife very well, but they had served on a board together a decade or so ago. Such a heartbreaking loss.

Sandy continued listening as she turned around and looked up to see Amy and Matt were watching her from the kitchen.

Sandy couldn't help but smile from what Jeff was telling her.

"No, Amy didn't tell me any of this," she glanced over at the kitchen. Amy hid behind Matt.

"But I'm so glad she didn't spoil this big surprise!" She glanced over at Amy who poked her head out from Matt's shoulder and smiled.

"Sure, yes . . . no, I agree. Yes, tomorrow morning works just fine. I'll be there at nine am."

She ended the call and looked down at her phone. Did that conversation just take place? Patterson farms was going to donate their venue to Harbor Ridge Community Church so that the Live Nativity could go on.

She walked over to the kitchen. This time she wasn't shooed away.

She held her arms open. "Thank you for this." Sandy let a tear leak from her eyes. Amy let out a smile.

They sat together to eat dinner. Fresh pineapple salsa, corn tortillas, veggies and pulled "pork" tacos made from jackfruit.

"Jack fruit?" Sandy asked as she looked around her plate.

Amy nodded as she took a bite of her taco. "Yes, it's a tree fruit."

Sandy wasn't so sure of this, but she took a bite of the crunchy taco anyway. Wow, it was delicious. She took another bite. And set it down. She took a sip of water.

She noticed Matt studying her reaction, "So what do you think?"

"It's different and not what I expected at all."

Amy lowered her head.

Sandy smiled, "But it's delicious. I like it a lot. Better than I thought I would. I never would have thought to try something like that."

Amy raised her head and looked at Matt who put his arm around Amy and pulled her close.

Sandy nodded at Amy. "You'll have to teach me how to make it."

"I'd like that," Amy smiled.

"Me too."

They had enjoyed a great dinner together, but she knew she needed to talk to Amy one on one. She knew Matt and Amy would be flying back out west in a few days. She knew they had to talk in person. So much always got lost in translation in text messaging. She had been trying so hard to connect with Amy and she knew this was her chance for them to start over. Matt had left to run an errand to pick up a Christmas gift.

She went up to Amy as they were cleaning up the kitchen. "Mind if we talk?"

Amy nodded as she continued to wipe down the counter.

"I can't thank you enough for talking to Mr. Patterson—Jeff. It's a good thing you didn't listen to me," Sandy laughed.

"I wasn't sure it would work out, but I wanted to try. I had to try. Matt told me how much the Nativity means to you. I think my mom would have loved it."

Sandy reached out to Amy's hand. She knew she had to speak from her heart. It wasn't easy to swallow her pride, but just like she felt the Holy Spirit at work in the frozen section of the grocery store, she felt the nudge here too.

"I haven't treated you in a way that I'm very proud of. And for that I am sorry."

Amy reached out and grabbed her hand. "I'm sorry too. I didn't know about all your traditions. I wasn't trying to replace anything."

Sandy smiled back at Amy.

"Ever since Matt was a little boy, I've thought about who he would marry someday. I prayed that it would be a special person who complimented Matt. Helped him grow and see the world differently. Someone who challenged him but didn't try to change him. I now know that that person is you, Amy. You are who I prayed for. I didn't see it at first. Selfishly I just didn't want him to grow up."

Amy blinked as tears fell from her face. Sandy reached her hands out to cup Amy's. "I thought I would know what this felt like because Matt's been away at college for four years, but honestly when I look at him, some days I still just picture my little blonde hair boy running around the house with a half-eaten apple in one hand and a plastic sword in the other. I'm sorry I haven't acted kindly toward you these past few weeks."

And with that, the weight that Sandy had been carrying washed away.

"I'm sorry, too. This is all new territory for me too. I do want you to know how much I love Matt. He's been such a great influence in my life. He saw things in me that I couldn't see in myself. I know that's because he had a wonderful mom."

Sandy smiled. They were good for each other, Matt and Amy. God has brought the two of them together and she had faith they would do great things together.

"I know your mom is in Heaven and I would never try to replace her. I never got to have any daughters but I'd love to build a special relationship with you if you would like."

"I'd love that. I thought after Christmas and before Matt and I fly back to school that you and I could go look at wedding dresses? If you're okay with us getting married?

"I would love that. I got to go with my niece a few years ago and my sister. It was a lot of fun. You are going to be a beautiful bride. I'd love to be included."

They embraced and Sandy couldn't help but smile.

Chapter Thirty-Four

Natalie walked into their office. Well now it was *her* office. Rachel's desk was empty. They were going to start interviewing candidates in the new year.

She looked up and saw Linda hovering over her desk. She would miss Linda's guidance and direction, but not her sneaky and unannounced visits. Linda tapped on Natalie's desk with her freshly manicured nails, "Natalie, do you have lunch plans this afternoon?"

Natalie shuffled the papers on her desk. "I, umm, was planning to work through lunch. With Rachel gone, I need to check on how the on-line auction is going." It wasn't a complete lie. She did need to follow up with some of the businesses to confirm when they could deliver the items to the auction winners.

"I see. Why don't we order lunch and meet in the conference room?"

Natalie looked down at her computer monitor to see the time. "Um, sure, okay. 11:30?"

Linda walked away and Natalie exhaled. Why did everything make her so nervous?

Natalie gathered her notebook and brought her laptop in the confer-ence room. Linda sat at the head of the table, regal as usual. As Natalie organized her thoughts on what to go over with Linda asked, "Natalie, what are your goals here?"

"I want to do a good job. I know it obviously wasn't anyone's first choice to have the festival canceled."

"I've noticed you here first thing in the morning and staying late. I've noticed how you talk with our vendors and how you've worked together with Rachel and other members of our team. The only thing I would ask of you is to have more confidence in yourself. I've seen you step up to the plate amidst the chaos going on right now. I know this must be stressful on you with Rachel gone and my retirement soon. But I think you're the perfect person to lead this group into the new year."

"What?" Natalie looked around the room.

"But here's the thing. You have to believe that you can. Do you believe you can?"

Natalie nodded. Linda stood up and walked out of the conference room.

* * *

Hannah sat at a corner table sipping on her hot apple cider while she waited for Natalie to arrive. It was her first morning off in quite some time. She had enjoyed Quinn and Luke's Christmas program at school and was taking some time to herself before conquering the house chores. Ben was supposed to be with her at the kids' school, but he got called away last minute for work. She could tell he felt bad about missing another performance. She stopped trying to pile on to the dad guilt he was feeling. It didn't do any good anymore, and he loved his job. She felt guilty about asking him to do something else. Still, she hated going to those events alone. She took another sip of her cider as she looked out the frosty window.

She watched as shoppers walked by the windows hurrying from one store to the next in search of the perfect present. She mentally went through her to-do list and realized the kids' teachers were the only gifts she had left to buy. After she met with Natalie, she would pop in across the street to get the kids' teachers a gift card. It would never be enough to show her gratitude for all the work they did. They were truly angels for all the hard work they did.

The door chimed and Hannah looked up, she saw Natalie walk in the diner. Her face slightly red from the blustery cold outside. Natalie walked over, took her coat and scarf off and hung them on the chair, and sat down, smiling.

"So tell me, are congratulations in order?" Hannah asked expectantly.

Natalie looked down at the table and bit her lower lip. "We'll see. I know HR still has to call and verify my references but I'm hopeful I'll start the new year in a new job." A smile spread over Natalie's face. Her eyes lit up. Her smile was contagious and Hannah couldn't help but smile back. She was so happy for her friend.

"Yes! That is very exciting. I'm happy for you. I know how hard you've worked."

Natalie stirred her hot chocolate. "I appreciate you being a reference. I know I left suddenly the other week but I just needed to figure some stuff out. I'd love to still babysit for the kids here and there."

"My mom used to always say, we all have our moments. We would love to have you come by whenever it works with your schedule. Or we can all just hangout together. I know they miss you."

"And by *all* hang out, who are you referring too?"

Hannah's eyes wandered about the perimeter of the room before asking what had been on her mind for weeks.

"Well Quinn and Luke of course. Would Eli be welcome to join us?" Hannah raised her eyebrow inquisitively.

"No." Natalie went back to reading her menu. "Something smells delicious. Is that sourdough?"

"Yes, they make all their bread fresh every morning. What happened between the two of you? You seemed happy together."

Hannah could see the sadness in Natalie's eyes.

"I'm sure he can fill you in. He kissed me."

Hannah's eyes tripled in size.

"What? When? How?"

"Slow down there." Natalie laughed and immediately looked like she wished she had not just disclosed that information.

"Was this after you broke up?"

"How can we break up if we were never really dating?"

"That's not what Quinn said."

Natalie laughed and shook her head. She didn't have any ill feelings toward Quinn about her observations. The truth was her and Eli had been flirty around the kids and she wouldn't deny it.

Hannah laughed. "So about this kiss?"

"We ran into each other at the gym and he came to step aerobics when I was subbing for Stepahnie."

Hannah's eyes widened. "I wish I could have seen that."

Natalie grinned at the memory. "It was quite entertaining. But at the end of class as we're putting away the equipment, we were talking about the past few months and then he kissed me."

Hannah's mouth fell to the floor.

"Wow. He didn't tell me any of this. He knows I would give him a hard time about it." Hannah's demeanor changed. "He is trying Natalie. Maybe you could give him the benefit of the doubt?"

Natalie couldn't help herself. "How's Amy?"

"Ouch. Sometimes relationships are beyond repair."

"I don't disagree."

Hannah nodded. She felt this nudging inside her heart. She'd felt it since the afternoon Amy showed up on her porch and again when Eli and Amy cornered her at the gym. A nudge that she knew what she needed to do but kept trying to ignore it. Kept trying to rationalize why she deserved to hold onto her anger. Hold on to feeling hurt. A prompting, probably the Holy Spirit, kept telling her to forgive. What was she waiting on? She gazed over at Natalie who's eyes held the same hurt feeling. Hannah had seen and talked to Eli and she knew Eli wanted to make amends with Natalie. How unfair of Natalie to not forgive him. *Exactly* she felt the Holy Spirit speak to her. *And how unfair of you to not forgive Amy.*

Chapter Thirty-Five

Eli walked up the icy driveway to Hannah's house. Every chance she got, Hannah gave him a hard time about Natalie not being able to babysit anymore, so when she asked if he could babysit, he said yes. Of course, getting to see his niece and nephew was an added bonus of choosing to live in Harbor Ridge. He was going to miss them when he moved. Hopefully he'd be able to visit them more than he had been. He was going to make sure of that.

"Uncle Eli, Uncle Eli!" Quinn and Luke exclaimed. He never grew tired of hearing them call his name. Or their big hugs.

They ran toward him with their arms opened wide. Eli exhaled as they were in his arms. Nothing about being in Harbor Ridge had turned out the way he wanted or expected except how his love for his niece and nephew grew. It was a gift for him to get to be a part of their lives. He felt a sadness come over him as he lingered in their embrace. Saying goodbye to them next month when he took on a new project . . . well he wasn't going to dwell on that now.

Quinn interrupted his thoughts, "What's wrong, Uncle Eli? Do you miss Natalie?"

Eli connected with her bright blue eyes and nodded. She tightened her hug. "It's okay. I miss her too."

He walked into the kitchen where Hannah and Ben were talking, they were opening their mail and going through the kids' backpacks.

As Hannah started sifting through the pile, she noticed a postcard. She held it up to Eli. "I thought you said they canceled the nativity?"

"They did, but they were able to find another location." Eli said as he took the flyer from her.

It read:

LOCATION CHANGE.
Patterson Farms
Dress warmly for the weather.

Eli smiled. A relief came over him. Mr. Patterson and Sandy had worked it out. Natalie was going to get the celebration she had worked so hard for.

Hannah re-read the flyer. "Wait—Patterson Farms? The farm that Dad's college roommate owned?

Eli nodded. "It is. We used to go there when we were younger, remember?"

Hannah smiled, "I do remember. Gosh, that was a long time ago." Eli could see the sadness move over her eyes and he knew she was reminiscing about their time with their parents.

"Amy and I went to talk to him. Amy came up with the idea to see if the farm was available and luckily they had a last-minute cancellation."

Hannah shrugged, "I didn't know Amy had time to think about anyone except herself."

Eli shot a look in her direction.

Hannah exhaled. "I'm sorry. That was nice of her I guess."

"Yes it was. Are you still taking the kids to the Festival?" Eli asked.

"If I don't have to work too late that night, but our neighbor Cheryl offered to take them with her kids if need be," she said.

"Unfortunately, I have to be in Richmond for a deposition that night," Ben added. "There's so much business going on to close the year out."

Hannah looked at Eli and rolled her eyes. He knew she was tired of Ben's crazy work schedule.

"I can take them if you want," Eli said.

Hannah looked at Eli curiously. "You did promise Quinn that you would be a shepherd, right?"

Eli laughed. "I suppose I did. And Quinn never forgets anything."

Hannah smiled, "No she doesn't."

Hannah's cell phone rang on the counter. Hannah walked over and removed it from the charger before answering.

"Hello . . . yes, this is her."

Hannah held up one finger to Eli as she slipped into the hallway. "I've known her for three years. Her greatest strengths? She is punctual and always helpful no matter what tasks. Her weakness? She can lack assertiveness. Anything else? Just that she's been a great employee and would make a fantastic addition to your team."

Hannah walked back into the kitchen.

"Who was that?"

Hannah looked around the room.

"Ben, we better hurry so we don't miss our dinner," she said.

"Be there in a few minutes," Ben spoke from his office.

Eli folded his arms. "Who called? It was about Natalie, wasn't it?"

Hannah folded her arms and mirrored Eli. "Yes but that's all I can tell you. Ask her yourself."

Eli ran his fingers through his hair. "I've tried and it hasn't done any good. Besides, I'm not sure where I'm going to be or what I'm going to be doing in the New Year. What's the point?"

Hannah uncrossed her arms and gave Eli a hug. She looked up at him.

"Hey. You don't have to have every little detail of your life figured out before you take a chance."

"I tried taking a chance and it didn't work out. Didn't even get off the ground. I've told you before, the holidays ruin so many relationships. Maybe something will change in the New Year but I am done."

"When does your new contract start?"

"I'm trying to decide between Colorado or Baltimore, but whichever one I pick will start the first week of February."

Hannah's lips turned downward. "That means there's zero chance you want to stay here?"

Eli shrugged. The truth was, he wanted to stay. Harbor Ridge had felt more like a home to him than anywhere else in a long time. He loved getting to spend time with his niece and nephew. But possibly running into Natalie and move on without dating her would be too much. It would be better for him to do what he always did, start over in a new city.

"You know me. I like to move around."

Hannah shook her head. "I thought maybe the kids had an impact on you and you would change your mind."

For the second time that day, Eli felt like the biggest jerk for leaving them again.

Chapter Thirty-Six

Natalie rubbed the side of her head as she went back to the parking lot. She had been on her feet the entire day setting up at the farm. She hoped they had a good turn out especially with the change of venue last minute. She stopped to pull a piece of gravel out of her shoe. She had been walking around with it for far too long as she carried items from her car in the parking lot to the farm which was going to house the Live Nativity. Three white tents had been donated for refreshments.

"Natalie, Natalie!" a familiar high-pitched voice called out.

Natalie looked up to see a white blob making its way over to her. As it got closer, under the lights, Natalie could see it was Quinn. She reached down to give her a hug. As they separated, Natalie noticed the white fuzz from Quinn's costume was stuck to her black pants. She laughed and she tried to brush it off.

"You look fantastic! Is your mom here?" she asked.

"No, Uncle Eli brought us."

A pit sat in Natalie's stomach. She had wanted to talk to him, but wasn't sure what to say. She looked up to see Eli walking toward them holding Luke's hand. He wore a baggy brown robe.

Natalie did her best to keep a straight face but a little smirk forced its way out.

"This looks incredible," Eli said.

"With no help from you," she responded.

Eli put his hand on her shoulder. "We should talk."

"Maybe later, I have a Live Nativity to run right now." Natalie took Quinn by the hand and walked away.

Eli followed closely behind with Luke.

Natalie held Quinn's hand as she got her and Luke to their spot in the Live Nativity. Another volunteer took control and made sure the children were all where they were supposed to be.

Natalie walked out of the barn and found an empty chair under one of the white tents. She checked on the refreshments and took a moment to take a break. She watched as the parking lot slowly began to fill with cars. She felt her heart rate pick up a few beats. It was almost showtime.

Amy walked over to Natalie and sat down next to her. Amy put her feet up in another seat in front of her stretching out her legs.

Amy tried to stifle a yawn. "I am exhausted and the first show hasn't even started yet."

Natalie laughed. "Me too. This has been one crazy week. I cannot believe we have almost pulled it off."

"Almost? Look around, Natalie—it's definitely been pulled off. You and Sandy and the team did an amazing job setting all of this up and being flexible. Something that I am definitely not."

Natalie smiled. "I guess I've learned to be flexible the older I've gotten. My dad always said, *"If you're flexible you can't get bent out of shape."*

Amy laughed. "That sounds like something my dad would say too. I miss him."

Natalie put her hand over Amy's and squeezed it. "I can't thank you enough for getting Mr. Patterson to let us use his farm. It's the perfect location. I can't believe we didn't think about using it before."

"Actually . . . oh, he's going to kill me when he finds out I told you."

Natalie was puzzled. "What are you talking about?"

Amy gritted her teeth. "I promised Eli I wouldn't say anything, but you should know. Eli went with me when I talked to Mr. Patterson about having the event here. Eli worked out the contract and gave it to Sandy. He made me promise to not tell you what he did."

Natalie's mouth opened. She shook her head, "Why would he do that?"

Amy smiled. "Well I can think of one reason he would." She winked at her.

Natalie couldn't believe it. "But why would he go to all that trouble after being the reason the city wouldn't let us have it outside the hospital?"

"You should go talk to him," Amy suggested.

Natalie slowly stood up from her chair, her knees wobbling making it difficult to walk. The sun had already set but the farm was illuminated by the spotlights they had set up and an impressive full moon that lit up the sky. She looked down at her watch and picked up her pace to try and talk to Eli before she had to be back at the Live Nativity to cue the choir. She couldn't be gone too long.

She rounded the corner and saw Eli. She couldn't wait to thank him for what he did to get the event moved.

Her heart dropped.

His back was turned and he was hugging a very attractive young woman. He turned and his eyes looked up and met Natalie's. Natalie felt the air get knocked out of her.

She quickly turned around to head back to the barn. She had no right to be jealous of him and who ever he was with. Sure he had kissed her last week, but what was that really even about? She had liked it though and was hoping to do that again. It didn't seem like that would be happening. He had already moved on.

* * *

Eli knew he had to go after her. "Natalie!" he called, his voice becoming more hoarse.

She turned around and met him.

"Eli, I don't want to do this now. Do this again. I can't."

He reached out for her hand to stop her. To his surprise, she turned back around to him.

"I let you walk away at the Chamber dinner and I wish I wouldn't have."

Natalie shifted her glance to the crowd he had just left.

"Who was that?" She tilted her head back to him.

"Who?"

Natalie rolled her eyes while avoiding eye contact with him. "The woman you were hugging just then."

Eli shook his head. "That's not what you think. She's an old friend. She's . . ."

Natalie's phone dinged. She took it out of her pocket and turned off the ringer.

"I'm needed at the front. The Nativity is about to begin. You need to be in your place with your costume."

Great. Were they ever going to get a chance to talk?

Eli watched as Natalie quickly made her way to the barn. He then made his way to his spot to join Quinn and Luke through the back entrance. Quinn couldn't contain her excitement when she saw Eli. Her smile brightened up the whole barn. She waved at Natalie and Natalie winked at her.

Eli stayed in character as a shepherd while shifting where he stood so he could watch Natalie on the sidelines. She had a black earpiece and microphone attached to her jacket where she was presumably talking to Sandy or the choir director to make sure the timing of everything went according to plan.

* * *

"Amy?" Natalie asked in the microphone. "You can let the rest of the guests in now. We have plenty of space to fill."

There was silence on the other end.

"Amy?"

"Natalie . . . I've let all the guests in."

Natalie lowered her head and rubbed the top part of her nose with her two fingers. There was this beautiful evening and not many people were going to show up for it. Had they gotten the word out to enough people?

Natalie took a deep breath and turned back to the Nativity. She saw smiling faces and kids kicking straw in the manger. She gave the go ahead for the choir to begin their medley of carols. As she became enthralled with the choir's rendition of "Angels We Have Heard on High," she felt eyes staring at the back of her head. She turned and her eyes met with Eli's.

"Natalie?"

Natalie put her hand on her earpiece. "Yes?"

"The parking lot is beginning to fill up. Are you ready for the next thirty guests?"

Natalie quickly scanned the room. Families were together and listening to the music and seeing the animals. They have space for more to join in.

"Yes, you can send them in."

Thanks, God. Just when it felt like no one would show up. Just when it felt like once again disappointment would reign. God was full of surprises.

All night a steady stream of visitors entered the farm for the Live Nativity. There were two shifts of workers. One for the first hour and one for the second hour. Some stayed for both. The line of visitors snaked around the building as they waited to be let in. The sound of the choir was audible from the outside and to Natalie's delight, the crowd also sang along.

In between the choir singing, Natalie passed her earpiece and clipboard to another volunteer so she could take a break to regroup. She found a quiet spot under the "volunteers only" tent. She paused to take it all in. Couples holding hands, families wrangling their children. Senior couples carefully walking together through the gravel parking lot. It was a beautiful night to celebrate the real meaning of Christmas. The gift of love, family and faith.

As she noticed a young couple holding hands, so clearly in love, a nagging feeling came over Natalie and as she usually did, her brain went to the *what if we had gotten married* scenario. What would life look like? What job would she be doing? Where would they live? Would she be happy?

She didn't think she would have been. No, she knew she wouldn't have been. She was about to stand up from the table to return to her shift.

Eli, still adorably dressed as a shepherd, walked over to her carrying two cups of hot apple cider. He handed one to Natalie.

"I figured you may want one of these to stay warm."

"Thank you." Natalie took it as he sat down next to her.

"But wait, you're from Michigan, so you're used to all of this cold, right?"

She smiled at him. He knew how to tease her. His tone changed. He took another sip of the warm apple cider and swallowed hard.

"The Monday after the Chamber dinner."

Natalie tried thinking back to when that was. Her mind was coming up blank. "What are you talking about?"

Eli scooted his chair closer to hers. He put his hand on her knee and connected his eyes to hers. "You asked me when I knew the city was cutting the funding on your event and that's when I knew. The Monday after our huge fight at the Chamber dinner. I mean, there had been whispers about it at meetings and even the night of the dinner, but I thought I had convinced them to keep it in the budget. I'm usually pretty convincing."

Natalie raised her eyebrow. Eli continued. "But it wasn't enough to backtrack on my report earlier for why I thought we should cancel it. I'm sorry."

Finally, his eyes showed what she had wanted all along. An apology. She didn't know how much she needed to hear that from him until she got it.

Eli continued, "We had just had this huge fight and I knew when you found out it would make everything worse. I wanted to tell you. I didn't want to hurt you. I didn't know the mayor was going to call Sandy before I got a chance to tell you. I wish I would have tried harder."

Natalie shared some of the blame in this. She wanted to know what had happened for their event to be canceled, but couldn't have the tough conversation. She wimped out when it came to confrontations.

"It wouldn't have mattered even if you had wanted to explain it to me. I wasn't responding to your texts." It seemed immature now, but she had been hurt and was angry. She needed time to process everything that was going on.

Eli took another sip of the warm apple cider. "You were right about what you said about Amy though at the Chamber dinner. We are talking again. I'm hopeful that will extend to Hannah at some point too."

"Amy told me that and I'm happy for you both. Time is such a gift and life is too short."

"She'll always be my sister. Thank you for encouraging me to talk to her."

Natalie nodded. "I don't know that I would say 'encouraged', more like 'insisted'. I can be a little pushy."

Eli nodded in agreement and Natalie laughed. She went back and forth in her head about whether to let him know she knew about how he had gotten the farm. She took a deep breath. "Amy told me that you helped her talk to Mr. Patterson about letting the church use their farm. Thank you."

She reached out and squeezed his free hand. He squeezed it back. "You're welcome." He stood up and embraced her in a hug.

Eli gazed around the outside of the farm. "I haven't been here since high school probably. This place had stayed the same. I enjoyed catching up with him."

"Amy mentioned your dad and Mr. Patterson went to college together?"

Eli nodded. "Yes they did. Their family and ours were close when we were growing up. I'm sure Amy told you our dads were roommates in college and started working at the same company. Our moms hit it off right away. We used to go to the beach together every year until we were in middle school and schedules got more complicated. The Pattersons had two girls and a son as well. That's who I was talking to tonight, by the way. Their daughter Julia. She was in the same grade as me and Hannah. She lives in Dallas, Texas now. She's an architect which makes sense, she was always drawing when we were kids. Tried to keep us all out of trouble. I took her to senior prom. She was the girl in the picture you found at my apartment."

"Ah I see. Reconnecting with your teenage crush?" Natalie teased him with a hint of sadness. They obviously had a long history together. She couldn't compete with that.

Eli winked at her. "I don't think Julia's husband would like that very much."

"Husband?"

"Yes, she's married and has a little boy. Her husband is driving in on Christmas Eve. He had to work tonight. Besides, he's a bodybuilder in his spare time. I'm pretty sure he could crush me."

Natalie brought her hand to her face. There was no way to block her face from becoming as red as her sweater. She had no reason to be jealous of Julia or anyone else Eli decided to date.

"I feel silly storming off the way I did. She probably thinks I'm a lunatic."

Eli squeezed her knee. "Nah, she knew you were just jealous. It happens to the best of us."

Natalie smiled. "Maybe a little."

They both stood up from their chairs at the same time. Natalie's phone buzzed in her pocket. She reached down and pulled it out.

"Five minute warning before I need to be back at the barn."

She turned to walk away and he gently grabbed her arm. She turned back and they were eye to eye.

"Look Natalie, I'm sorry about what I said to you the night of the Chamber dinner. I know it's not an excuse but I had a lot of stress on my plate that night and you just happened to be in the wrong place. I apologize."

I guess I should tell him.

"You weren't wrong, either. I was using my past as an excuse to avoid any more rejection and life just doesn't work that way. Rejection is a part of life. I was keeping myself from being happy."

Eli nodded. "I hated seeing you letting some dumb guy make you feel like you couldn't live the life you deserved. You are incredibly talented and deserve the best."

Natalie smiled. "Thank you. I took your blunt and frankly needed advice and applied for a new job and got it. I start the first of the year."

Eli's eyes widened, "You're moving?"

"No, I'm not. It's still with the hospital but I'll be managing their staff of volunteers. Get to plan events and outreach programs. The best part is that I get to take some time off before my new job starts so I'm going to meet up with my parents for Christmas but I'm not flying out until Christmas Day."

Eli put his arms around her and gave her a side hug. "Amy told me why this event is so important to you. How you always dreamed of having a December wedding. I understand why you didn't want to tell me, but I wish you would have. I'm sorry that happened to you."

"Thank you. Maybe someday I'll stop being embarrassed about it."

"You have nothing to be embarrassed or ashamed about. I hate the thought of anyone ever hurting you."

Natalie exhaled. "It did hurt, more than I'd like to admit. I think I kept hurting myself by not moving on. By not believing in myself anymore."

Eli looked down. "I'm not sure if I should tell you this or not, but you know how we got the farm, right?"

"Yeah, Amy told me you and her went and talked to Mr. Patterson and connected him with Sandy."

Eli put his arms on her shoulders. "Well yes that's part of it, but Natalie, we asked him if we could use the farm nine days ago. The only reason he was able to say yes was because they had a last-minute cancellation."

"Wow, that was lucky. Well, more than luck. I think we both know who had a hand in that."

"We do." Eli nodded. "But look, Natalie, there was supposed to be a wedding here tonight and it was canceled last minute."

Natalie sucked in air. She felt bad for everyone involved. She knew what having to undo a wedding entailed and how hurtful it was.

Natalie looked up at him. "Why did you tell me this now?"

He looked over at her. "I wanted to tell you, because I wanted you to know that sometimes good can come from hard situations, even if we don't see it." His eyes were soft with concern.

"Wow," was all Natalie could say at that moment.

Eli hung his head. She quickly stood up and started walking away. She turned back to him.

"One more thing," she said. She walked back over to him, stood on her tiptoes and kissed him.

"Could you wait for me?"

Eli smiled. "Yeah."

She couldn't help but smile as she walked back over to the nativity.

* * *

Hannah finished her shift earlier in the evening and decided to catch the last hour of the nativity so she could see the kids dressed up.

She was surprised to see the parking lot was still full. A nice gentleman dressed in a reflector vest walked with her to the front of the farm across the gravel lot.

She was greeted by two cheerful women wearing Harbor Ridge Church buttons who opened the doors to the barn. She stepped into the venue and it immediately took her breath away.

At that moment she forgot about the dishes she needed to do at home, how sore her feet were from the hours of walking the hallways of the hospital, and the pressure of scheduling family visits during Christmas. As she walked the path of the Live Nativity, she passed the shepherds. She waved to Eli, who did not break character but said hello with his eyes.

She came to the manger scene. On top of the balcony was a little girl wearing a white dress and shiny halo that twinkled under the spotlight. Her smile was even brighter. Hannah couldn't help but smile too.

Lying underneath a giant silver star was the Christ child.

The choir director led the choir of angels in an a cappella version of "Hark the Herald Angels sing."

God and sinners reconcile.

Quinn and Luke were sitting at the feet of Mary and Joseph. Quinn's eyes caught her mother's and she yelled out "Mama, Mama!"

Hannah smiled and waved.

She walked around the rest of the barn and saw the camels and donkeys. She was too enthralled by the production of it all to notice the smell.

She stood in awe of the scene before her. The choir continued to sing in the background on risers. Her mom would have loved this. Hannah continued to listen to the choir and almost serendipitously they began to sing "Joy to the World." Her mom's favorite Christmas song.

Hannah paused as she reflected. For the first time in a long while, she allowed herself to remember the last Christmas they shared as a family with her parents at their house. Everyone was there. It was two days after Christmas. They had spent the night before so Quinn and Luke could wake up and Santa could come. Her mom always did such a beautiful job of sharing the good works of Saint Nicolas. It was never confusing to her as a child who Christmas was actually for. Santa just added into the fun. Christ was always the center of their Christmas.

Her parents never cared whether they came on the actual day of Christmas or if it was before or after. All that mattered to them was that the entire family was together. Her mom went to wake up Amy who reluctantly got out of bed. That was the rule. No one could open gifts until everyone was downstairs. Eli made coffee. Hannah could smell the aroma of the strong brew, the way Eli liked it and everyone else tolerated. All the adults needed extra caffeine to keep up with the two lively toddlers.

Hannah escaped to the kitchen to warm up her cup and her mom came up beside her, giving her a hug. "Did you have a good Christmas?" Hannah yawned and then laughed. Her mom yawned too. "You gotta stop that. We're just getting started." They both smiled. "This is wonderful, Mom. Thank you. It wouldn't be Christmas without being here."

"I love Christmas." Her mom walked over to the manger scene on the mantle in their dining room. It was wooden. Luke liked to play with it and frequently rearranged the people. Hannah's mother didn't mind. Her house was always kid friendly.

Hannah walked over still clutching her warm coffee mug. She took a sip. "I've always loved this one. Well, all of the ones you have, but this one is my favorite."

"How so?" her mother asked inquisitively.

"It's the simplest of all of them. Plus I don't stress that the kids can break it. They seem pretty durable."

"It's pretty amazing isn't it? To think that the first Christmas was in a barn."

Hannah nodded. A scream stole her attention as she turned to see Quinn and Luke fighting over a toy. Luke snatched it and began to run away from Quinn. Quinn quickly stood up and ran after him. Eli stepped in and grabbed Luke, while Amy grabbed Quinn.

"Guys! Calm down."

"Wow this takes me back," Hannah's dad said as his eyes moved from the grandchildren to his adult children.

"I don't know what you're talking about. We were always well behaved." Eli smirked while wrangling a squirmy toddler.

"Yeah right," Mrs. Collins put her hand on her hip. "Oh the stories I could tell."

"Yeah, but look at how we turned out. All close," Amy said. Eli and Hannah nodded. And it was true. They had a text thread they sent inside jokes and updated each other about their lives weekly. They genuinely enjoyed each other's company.

Her parents embraced each other. "And that is what we always prayed for. That the three of you would remain close."

"Always." Hannah said.

Hannah felt a hand on her back as she came out of her reverie. She turned around and gasped.

"I can't believe you made it! What about your meeting tomorrow morning?"

Ben gently brushed a tear off her cheek. "I told them I could do a virtual call . . . after the holidays. I drove straight from the airport. I'm so glad

I made it in time."

He put his hands on her cheeks and kissed her. Hannah felt her knees go weak.

"You did what?" Hannah couldn't believe what she heard. For years she had been asking Ben to set better work boundaries and hours. She knew it wasn't always up to him, but as the kids got older they noticed he wasn't around as much. Ben had finally compromised with her. She couldn't believe he was standing next to her. She hugged him again as if she were to let go, he'd disappear.

"Are you ready to go home?" he asked her.

Hannah looked around another time at the Living Nativity to soak it in. She felt a nagging in her chest. She reached in her pocket and pulled out her keys. She held them out to him. "Can you take the kids home? There's something I need to do." They switched keys.

"Of course," he answered.

Hannah began to walk around the perimeter of the venue. The volunteers were beginning to clean up. The crowd began to thin out as children were being picked up. Hannah noticed Natalie walking around carrying a clipboard, methodically checking off boxes. Hannah tapped her on the shoulder. Natalie jumped.

"I'm so sorry. I didn't mean to scare you." Hannah wiped her face again with the sleeve of her jacket.

"It's fine. I'm just a little over-caffeinated. It's been a long day." Natalie hesitated. "A long few months, actually. Are you okay?"

Hannah turned her head to take in the Living Nativity one more time. "This was beautiful. I've never seen anything like it. It was a special night. I haven't taken the kids to anything like this before." She turned back to Natalie. "Now I want to make it our yearly tradition."

Mirroring Hannah's emotions, Natalie's eyes filled with tears. "It still gets me every year. I forget how beautiful the manger is and the angel. Good news of great joy. The sounds of the choir adds to the emotion of it all. It's easy to get distracted by all the other stuff but this is what matters."

Hannah nodded. "This is what matters."

Natalie smiled. "The kids were great. They nailed their parts. And Eli?" she laughed. "Well he is just full of surprises."

"Have you seen him lately? Did he go home already?" Hannah asked.

Natalie hesitated. "He's outside under the white tent. Natalie paused and as if to say with a warning, "He's with Amy. She came to help me and Sandy tonight."

Hannah nodded. "Thanks."

Hannah took her time walking to the tent. The deal she had made with herself was that if Amy was still here, she would talk to her. It was overdue. Still, she was scared. Her pulse quickened and she thought about what she wanted to say. Her stomach felt like it was in her chest.

So much wasted time.

There were several tables set up with hot apple cider, coffee, and baked goods to feed the volunteers. Poinsettias sat in the middle of the tables on top of white tablecloths. There were several families gathered around the tables as the evening came to a close.

Hannah stood from afar and watched the families all interacting together. They were smiling and sharing snacks. She noticed Eli and Amy sitting opposite each other in the corner of one of the tents. They were laughing. Her emotions began to bubble to the surface. Great—she was crying before she even got a word out. As she came closer to the tent, Eli noticed her and their eyes met. A look of concern in his eyes. He was probably wondering if there was going to be some confrontation like before. Hannah shifted her glance to Amy as Amy quickly diverted her eyes. Hannah walked toward her. Hannah's voice barely made out a whisper.

"Amy?"

Amy turned back to her. "Don't worry, I'll leave you alone so you and Eli can talk. We're about to head home anyway."

Amy stood up from her chair. As she walked in the different direction, Hannah cut across the table. She didn't know what to say except to open her arms. The wall between them, finally broken. Hannah could barely muster a whisper. "Please don't go. Please. You don't have to run away anymore."

Amy put her face in her hands. Her shoulders shook with emotion.

As she pulled her hands away from her face, her eyes overflowing with tears she whispered, "I'm so sorry."

Hannah wrapped her arms around her, gently stroking her back as they both sobbed.

"Me too," Hannah said. "Me too."

Amy pulled back and wiped both eyes with her fingers. "I didn't think you'd be here. Eli told me you weren't coming." She motioned to Eli who was himself trying to keep his emotions at bay.

"I wasn't sure I was going to get off work in time. I'm so glad I did. Quinn has been wearing her sheep costume all week." Hannah smiled warmly as she sniffled.

Eli waddled over still in his shepherd costume trying not to trip on his hem.

"You look ridiculous," Amy kidded him. The three of them laughed.

He shrugged. "Anything for Quinn or Luke."

"That's sweet. She has you wrapped around her finger."

"What can I say? I'm doomed." Hannah and Amy laughed.

The three of them embraced in a group hug. They continue talking about catching up.

Hannah looked around the farm, memories flooded back. "How did you remember and know to ask Mr. Patterson? I never would have thought of using his farm. It's changed so much."

Amy looked around. "I remembered coming to his farm when we were kids. We used to swim in the pool during the summer and ride horses. It was the highlight of my summer."

Hannah asked, "I thought you had blocked everything out about living in Harbor Ridge."

Amy clutched her chest. "It hurt too much to think about. Everything we lost. Mom and Dad will never hold my babies. They won't get to see me get married. I guess I just felt so jealous that you got to have them for all of those things but I didn't. That wasn't fair to you. I'm sorry."

"You're right, it wasn't fair. I was hurting, too."

Hannah looked down at the ground. "But I should have thought about how it affected you. I wish you would have talked to me about it. I wish I could have understood."

Amy took a sip of her drink. "It almost felt healing in a way talking to Mr. Patterson. It was the first time in a long long time that I've been able to think about Mom and Dad and not be sad. To finally be able to focus on good memories."

"You're healing." Hannah smiled.

"We all are," Eli chimed in.

Eli and Hannah hugged.

Matt and Natalie joined the group after finishing some clean up.

"Well that is a wrap for this year's celebration. I feel like I could sleep until the New Year," Natalie said as she sat down in one of the chairs.

"That makes two of us." Hannah laughed.

Natalie looked at Matt. "Thanks again for helping people get from the parking lot to the barn. I was worried someone might fall, but knock on wood we had no injuries tonight."

"You're welcome. It was worth it to see my mom so happy. She really loves this event."

"Where is she? I haven't gotten a chance to see how the auction went?"

Matt smiled and gestured over to the barn. His mom and Mr. Patterson were engrossed in conversation with big smiles on both of their faces. Mr. Patterson pointed out different parts of the barn before they both walked over.

"It's wonderful to see you all together. Your parents would be so proud of the adults you have become. I know your mom would be especially pleased with this event. She was all about Christmas."

Hannah smiled. "She definitely was. We have her tree in our living room now. It's always fun to reminisce about all the old ornaments. Such great memories. Mr. Patterson, it is so nice to see you again."

Sandy gave him a side hug, "Thank you again for letting us use your farm. We couldn't ask for a better location."

Mr. Patterson nodded. "I couldn't have asked for a better friend than Mr. Collins."

Sandy said, "And, Mr. Patterson said we could use this venue next year."

Natalie added. "That's fantastic. Now we don't have to involve the city again." She gave a look toward Eli.

Mr. Patterson added. "Let's discuss it over coffee in the New Year. Maybe there's more ways we can put the barn to use."

Sandy smiled bigger than Natalie had ever seen. "That would be lovely."

Mr. Patterson held his arm out for Sandy to grab as he escorted her to the parking lot. Amy eyed Matt as Mr. Patterson helped Sandy carry some boxes to her car.

"Well, this night just continues to be full of surprises." Amy laughed as she elbowed Matt.

"Hey, I just want Mom to be happy. She deserves all the happiness in the world after everything she's given to me."

Amy nodded in agreement.

"I've got to go finish packing up some of the equipment. I'll meet you back here at nine?"

Amy nodded. Matt kissed her forehead.

"I'll see you on Friday night." Hannah turns to Amy. "I don't know what your plans are for Christmas, but we'd love to have you over if you want. We have so much to catch up on."

"I would love that," Amy hugged Eli and Hannah.

Hannah gazed around the farm. She finally spotted Matt serving an elderly lady with a cup of hot chocolate. He smiled at her and she smiled back while giving a nod.

"You're welcome to bring Matt too. I'd love to get to know him."

Amy twisted the ring around her left ring finger and smiled while looking down at it. "Thanks, me too."

Hannah gives Amy a side hug.

Hannah turned to Eli. "What is Natalie doing for Christmas? Is she still going to Texas?"

"Yes. Her flight leaves on Christmas Day."

Hannah put her hand on Eli's shoulder. "Have you decided about the job?"

Eli shrugged and shook his head. Hannah squeezed his shoulder. "You've got to decide before the deadline."

"I know I do."

Chapter Thirty-Seven

Natalie put her coffee mug down on her table and stood up to answer the door. She pushed her suitcase out of the way to look through the peephole before quickly glancing around her apartment. She was glad she had decided to tidy up before leaving to catch her flight. She went over to the mirror to glance at her reflection and fix her hair.

She heard another knock and quickly went to open the door.

Eli looked up from the floor as they made eye contact. "Hi," he said warmly as he shifted his messenger bag to his other shoulder.

"Hey." After a few moments, Natalie broke the awkward pause. "Would you like to come in?"

Eli nodded as he followed her into her apartment.

"I wasn't sure if you'd be home. I know you said you have a flight to catch. Me too."

Natalie moved a blanket out of the way and motioned for him to sit down on the couch. He glanced up at the television and rolled his eyes. "Amy and Hannah were watching this before I left."

He looked back at Natalie. "Which is the only reason I tolerated it being on. That they were both watching something together. Finally." He laughed as he scratched the side of his face. "It's nice for them to be able to be in the same room again together."

Natalie nodded. "I'm glad."

"Me too."

Eli looked around her apartment. "Wow! You certainly went all out for Christmas, didn't you?"

Natalie smiled. "I know it's not your thing, but I like it."

"So how do you feel about us being neighbors for a little longer? I just renewed my lease for another year."

Natalie wasn't sure what to make of what he just said. His contract with the city was ending soon and he was heading to another project . . . or so she'd thought. "Next year's lease?"

Eli nodded. "Yeah, I'm going to stay in Harbor Ridge."

"What? Are you staying on at the Chamber?"

"Not in an official capacity, but maybe as a board member in the Spring. We'll see."

"So what will you be doing exactly?"

El unzipped the outer pocket of this bag and pulled out a brochure. "You're going to think I'm crazy."

"I already do." Natalie grabbed the paper in his hand.

Natalie started opening the brochure as Eli explained. "In Nashville, we had several indoor playgrounds for kids with tons of space for them to run around. Luke and Quinn loved them when they came to visit. Harbor Ridge doesn't have anything like this within thirty miles. I'm going to open a franchise here."

"This looks amazing. Luke and Quinn will love it. But didn't you spend the last few months writing reports about why businesses shouldn't come to Harbor Ridge?"

He sighed. "Yes, but I also saw what Harbor Ridge could be with what you and Sandy and Mr. Patterson pulled off. It's a town about people and I want to be a part of it. Hannah's family is here. Amy and Matt want to move here next year. I see a future here. Besides this town has something else. You."

Natalie exhaled. "Wow, I was not expecting that."

Eli reached down and pulled out a gift bag from his backpack. "I got you something."

"What is this?"

"Open it."

Natalie took it hesitantly. "Wait, I thought you didn't do Christmas gifts. Something about it sending the wrong signal or something?"

"I've been sending signals left and right."

Natalie smiled and brushed the hair behind her ear feeling her cheeks become flushed. "Really? I hadn't noticed," she answered sarcastically.

He nodded as he gestured to the bag with the colorful ribbon. He had obviously plucked it from Hannah's endless stash.

Natalie recognized the ribbons holding the bag handles together. "Did Hannah help you with this?"

He smiled sheepishly. "Just with the wrapping, not with the gift."

Natalie slowly unwrapped the tissue paper. She unwrapped a beautiful snow globe.

She recognized the scene inside the snowy globe. It was of Mary, Joseph, and the baby Jesus. She felt tears coming to her eyes.

"It's from the diner where we ate after the children's musical?"

He nodded. "Yep, it was a part of the basket the diner donated to the Festival of Trees. Their tree was my favorite."

Natalie playfully punched him in the shoulder. "Wait, not only did you go to the Festival of Trees but you also *bid* on something?"

"I did."

Natalie laughed. "Wow. Thank you. I love it."

"And who knows, maybe next year I'll even sponsor a tree?"

Natalie grinned. She scooted closer to him on the couch as he wrapped his arm around her shoulder. Eli started humming along to "Santa Claus is Comin' To Town" that was playing as the ending credits rolled on the movie on the television.

Natalie giggled as she looked up at him, "So is it safe to say Eli Collins finally likes Christmas?"

He looked down at her, "Maybe, but not as much as I like you."

She set the snow globe down on her coffee table. His hand caressed her cheek and he gently kissed her.

"Can I give you a ride to the airport?"

Natalie's demeanor turned serious, "I'm still not sure how I feel about your driving."

He laughed and then pulled her closer. She looked up to him as a smile spread across her face. This was the best Christmas yet.

About the Author

Melissa Sneed Wilson is the award-winning author of *Growing Up and Going Back*. A communications professional and adjunct professor, Melissa enjoys writing stories that are relatable, inspirational, and hope-filled. She placed in the semifinals for the Kairos Prize for Uplifting Screen Plays in 2009 and 2012 for her scripts, *Whose You Are* and *Castle in the Sand*. Melissa received a Bachelor's of Arts in Communications and Spanish from Carson-Newman University and a Masters in Professional Communication from East Tennessee State University.

She currently lives in Blountville, Tennessee with her husband and their two children.

She'd love for you to connect with her at:

🐦 MelissaSWilson

📘 melissasneedwilson